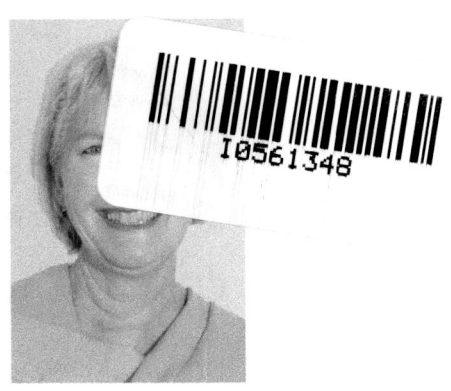

Karen grew up in a small country town in north-eastern Victoria, Australia. She spent her childhood riding horses through beautiful scenery of eucalypts, lakes, and snow-capped mountains and her love of landscape deeply affects her writing. She worked in a range of educational settings and holds a Ph.D. and M.Ed. (Hons) in the areas of fantasy. She is particularly interested in the power of the hero's inner journey which she explores through Deep Fantasy. Karen has travelled extensively overseas but enjoys nothing more than camping in the Australian Outback. She lives in Melbourne and now writes full-time. You can find out more about Karen and her books on her website.

Connect with K. S. Nikakis

Amazon: https://www.amazon.com/author/ksnikakis
Twitter: https://twitter.com/KSNikakis
Facebook: www.facebook.com/ksnikakis
Goodreads: www.goodreads.com
Website: www.ksnikakis.com
Email: author@ksnikakis.com

WORKS BY K S NIKAKIS

Non Fiction

Journey: Seeking the Sacred, Spirit and Soul in the
Australian Wilderness

Fantasy Novels
Series

Angel Caste series:
Angel Blood
Angel Breath
Angel Bone
Angel Bound
Angel Blessed
Angel Caste – Complete 5 Book Series

The Kira Chronicles trilogy:*
The Whisper of Leaves
The Song of the Silvercades
The Cry of the Marwing
remnant hard copies only

The Kira Chronicles series:
The Whisper of Leaves
The Silence of Stone
The Secrets of Stars
The Thunder of Hoofs
The Crying of Birds
The Music of Home
The Kira Chronicles – Complete 6 Book Series

Fantasy Novels

The Emerald Serpent
Heart Hunter
The Third Moon
Messenger
I Heard the Wolf Call My Name
Finalist Best YA Novel Aurealis Awards, 2019

Fantasy Short Stories

The Gift
The Tale of Prince Anura
Dragon Sprite
Glass-Heart
Finalist Best YA Short Story Aurealis Awards, 2019

Angel Caste Book 4
Angel Bound

K.S.Nikakis

Angel Caste – Book 4 Angel Bound

First published by SOV Media Australia 2017
Amazon: www.amazon.com.au

Angel Caste series - Book 4 Angel Bound © copyright by
KS Nikakis 2017

Publisher: SOV Media
Melbourne, Australia.

Cover by AS Nikakis: http://asnikakis.com
Shutterstock.com/ schankz
DaFont.com/Abdullah Alkhafaji – Ghost Theory 2

National Library of Australia
Cataloguing-in-Publication entry:
Nikakis, Karen Simpson
The Angel Caste series – Book 4 Angel Bound
ISBN 978-0-6489797-7-7

Learn more about KS Nikakis and her deep fantasy
books at: www.ksnikakis.com

For the Terang Gang – Helen and Tony Barton

Glossary of the Rynth

ANGEL CASTE

Crystal Fold
Principae (*prin-sip-ay*)
Nearest to ultimate transcendence. Manifest mainly as aqua light, with white wings and group consciousness. The Principae transcend Crystal Fold to the Great Beyond.

Ezam Fold
Archae (*ar-kay*)
Five levels: angels ascend from Quin-archae through Quar-archae, Tri-archae, Du-archae, Prime-archae to Archae. The Archae transcend Ezam Fold to Crystal Fold to become Principae, then transcend to the Great Beyond.

Members of the Archae
Archae Kald
Archae Dejon (*day-jon*)

Members of Prime-archae
Prime-archae Mirek
Prime- archae Serith

Dane
Lowest in the hierarchy and newest angels to Ezam. Ascend from Dane to Quin-archae, and then through the hierarchy to Archae to eventually transcend to Crystal Fold as Principae, and then to the Great Beyond.

Members of Dane
Thrisdane
Kydane (*kie-dane*)
Ashdane

DAIMON CASTE
Reside in any fold where angel caste has joined with other castes and produced offspring. The term is also used for those who have *any* angel caste heritage.

Moonsun Fold
Viv Wright

Wheel Fold – females - elddra; males - elddric

Elddra
Anfarena – most senior (*an-far-reena*)
Anetherey (*a-neth-er-ray*)

Elddric
Baraghan – surgeon/healer (*bara-gan*)

HUMAN CASTE

Moonsun Fold
Members of Human Caste
Lettie Wright – Viv's mother
Jimmy (Ronald James) Wright – Lettie's husband
Rim (Rimmon) – gang leader

Wheel Fold
Scharii – travelling musicians (*shar-ree*)

Members of the Scharii
Tarchen en-Scharii (*tar-chen*)
Darch en-Scharii

About Wheel Fold: The eight sectors or Vales of Wheel Fold. The eight sectors of Wheel Fold are: Eshavale, Ascavale, Warinavale, Genessavale, Beshavale, Terissavale, Sonoravale and Morvavale. These run north-south or cloudwise-starwise from the hub/peak: Astraal. The lake and city are also called Astraal. Each Vale has countless smaller valleys or vals. Each Vale has a main river eg Eshavale – Eshacade; Ascavale - Ascacade etc. Settlements near the river take their name from the river eg Esh-embrin; Esh-accom. The tributaries that flow from the vals are rills. Smaller settlements (setts) take their name from the rills eg Scinta-ril (on the Scinta Rill). Inhabitants of these setts are identified by their sett eg Ataghan en-Scinta-ril; Sehereden en-Scinta-ril.

Directions
Cloudwise – north
Starwise – south
Nightwise – west
Sunwise - east

Time Divisions
Zadicans (years) are divided by zadics of 45 days that include a period of recalibration in between (Vorash). Zadics are marked by constellations which appear and disappear in the night sky. Each has a particular meaning.

The zadics are: Pool, Cascade, Fire, Ice, Lirium, Glimwing, Cadestone and Horse. Other brief zadics (Call Zadics), are meaningful to individuals and indicate the individual should visit the sacred city.

Eshavale – Vale of Wheel Fold

Members of the Eshadi
Ataghan en-Scinta-ril – Syld, band leader, lein to Sehereden (*ata-gan*)
Sehereden en-Scinta-ril – lein to Ataghan, member of Ataghan's band (*se-hera-den*)
Fariye – choose-daugher of Ataghan (*far-re-ay*)
Brithergen – member of Ataghan's band
Jethren – member of Ataghan's band
Anthran – member of Ataghan's band
Daran – member of Ataghan's band
Sandagh – member of Ataghan's band (*san-da*)
Inaghan – member of Ataghan's band (*in-a-gan*)
Tormis – server in Ataghan's compound in Esh-accom
Mereya - server in Ataghan's compound in Esh-accom
Sirenya – Fariye's mother (deceased)

Caibel – unacknowledged son of Baraghan (*kay-bel*)
Galian – choose brother of Ithreya

Eshadi Sylds (acknowledged leaders)
Ataghan en-Scinta-ril
Darthen en-Within-ril
Mathian en-Fessen-ril
Garath en-Moss-ril
Kurnen en-Vara-ril

Valen Setts (communities)

Tahsin's Sett
Tahsin – sett leader (*tar-sin*)
Enesha – harvester (*ee-nesh-a*)
Prenya – cook (*pren-ya*)
Borash – cook
Fahan – harvester – twin brother of Merhen (*fay-han*)
Merhen – harvester – twin brother of Fahan (*mer-han*)
Doran – guard, kitchen helper
Cazir – harvester, guard (*kaz-eer*)
Jered – harvester, guard

Amethen's Sett
Amethen – sett leader (am-a-then)
Drasen – band leader
Ithreya – sett member (*ith-ray-a*)

Stonash – a small people with hooded eyes, flattened faces, and leathery skin - urrut traders
Long-arms – long-armed kin of the Stonash

LEFER CASTE

Wheel Fold
Lefer Caste are bird/bat-like beings with human caste-like intelligence

Members of Lefer Caste
Roaith en-Leferen – blue crest (*ro-aith*)
Garian en-Leferen – red crest – alpha of the Rookery.

BEASTMAN CASTE
Beastman Fold
Beastmen are puma-human mix creatures with human caste-like intelligence

IDIOMATIC EXPRESSIONS COMMON IN AUSTRALIA

Viv is Australian, and uses a range of idiomatic expressions.

Keep tabs on – check on; monitor
Didn't wash/did wash – didn't/did sound true; wasn't/was acceptable
On the line – to take a risk/be at risk
Knocked-up – made pregnant; being pregnant
Get out of jail free card – from a board game where a special card grants the player advantages
Second chance draw – another ticket is picked out from the losing tickets in a lottery
Sticks the boots in – attacks physically or verbally
Dodged the honesty bullet – to 'dodge a bullet' is to escape something bad
Brownie points – points awarded by doing good deeds that will eventually grant a reward (from the junior group in the Girl Guides movement)
Take the cake – win the prize
Druggies – drug addicts
Sh*t hits the fan – something bad happening with widespread effects

Angel Caste Book 4
Angel Bound

Chapter 1

The weather remained fine and Viv was pleased that the small party from Amethen's sett made good time. Even Nurana seemed to have relaxed and Drasen and Ithreya made for pleasant company. Viv was still keen for the journey to end. The sooner she reached Esh-accom and farewelled Poss, the sooner she would be on her way to her mother, wherever she was.

As they rode the next morning, Viv began to wonder if her luck had finally changed. They had not needed to seek shelter from Soaich's Bolts or from stray Waradi intent on avenging their leader's death. Her stomach clenched and Sehereden reached back and briefly touched her leg. Fara had transmitted her upset to him and Viv dragged her thoughts back to her surroundings, and her surroundings were not bad at all. The sun was warm, birds skittered in the trees, and she grudgingly admitted she enjoyed Sehereden's proximity.

Riding without harness meant she rested against him and the physical contact was like a balm after the long days of loneliness. She felt protected, as if Sehereden formed a barrier between her and the world. Beware the myth of the Prince in shining armour, she reminded herself cynically, *and* of Fara raising Sehereden's expectations he would soon be enjoying her *gifts* along with Ithreya's.

Sehereden seemed to have taken on Ithreya's role of tour guide, taking pains to describe things as they rode, but Viv knew he worked to rebuild her trust. He had suggested last night he wanted more than a passing fling but Viv did not know what that meant. The men's interest in sex seemed heightened by Fire Zadic as did the women's, but did it all die away afterwards and couples go their separate ways?

When she had sheltered in libraries as a fourteen-year-old, she had read of tribes who only had sex to conceive children, but the way Ithreya had drooled over Sehereden at Amethen's sett did not suggest it, nor did the fact she continued to seek sex with him and that he was happy to oblige.

And where did lein-trysting fit in? Was it just a temporary arrangement for Fire Zadic? Given leinships were permanent, lein-trysts probably were too, and must be exclusive, or else she could see no point in them, unless they provided *undisputed* claims to children.

And of all the strange things she had come across since leaving home, the men's want for children was the strangest. She was used to men who deserted their pregnant girl friends or demanded they abort, or deserted established families to start new ones. At best, they saw children as an inconvenience, and at worst, as a financial impost they refused to pay for, especially if they wanted to spite their former partner. None of it mattered, given she was not going to hang around, and yet she dreaded going on alone, and again Sehereden reached back and used his touch to reassure her.

They stopped at midday to eat and Viv was glad to stretch her legs. No fires were lit, the group spreading out to pick purplish berries from a stand of glossy-leaved bushes instead. Viv joined in, delighting in the berries' sweetness, but soon discovered the underside of the innocent-looking leaves delivered a nasty burn.

She flicked her hand but the sear grew. 'Scorch-berries only grow in starwise vals,' said Sehereden, suddenly beside her 'and these ones are early,' he added as he took her hand sucked the wound. Viv would have been embarrassed had her hand not been on fire. The sear eased but he did not move away. 'I didn't realise you were unfamiliar with the *starwise* vals or I would have warned you.'

If Sehereden expected her to confirm she came from a *cloudwise* val, he was to be disappointed. 'Thank you for your aid,' she said briefly, intent on her hand. 'If you'd told me what to do, I would have sucked it myself, or dipped it in the rill.'

'Only saliva quenches scorch-berry burns and mine's more effective than yours,' he said, still intent on her.

Viv looked at him in surprise, thinking he was joking. 'How do you know that?'

'Experience,' he said obscurely, and glanced at those still picking. 'Come, I'll show you how to harvest safely.'

Viv did not need many berries to feel full, and neither did the rest of the party, given they were soon mounted and on their way. The rill bubbled along beside them, and Sehereden's conversation continued, now aimed at eliciting information about her likes, dislikes, and wants for the future. He shared things about himself too, and

Viv learned his father had been a cloth-wright, and he had been raised in a cloudwise sett on the Even Rill.

'My mother and father were lein-trysted,' he explained.

'So, you've got brothers and sisters?'

'Not seed ones, which is why sett's discourage lein-trysts.' He smiled. 'Lein-trysts don't always deliver what they promise, although what they promise is precious indeed.' He paused. 'My mother suffered much illness and my father was later gifted choose-children.'

Viv got the impression Sehereden disapproved of his father's faithlessness and did not see his father's choose-children as siblings but it still reinforced that *all* children were wanted and she sighed. If only Jimmy Wright and Kald had come from *this* fold!

'Did your mother speak to you of your seed-father?' he asked.

'No,' said Viv, suddenly cautious.

'That must have been hard for you. Even when mothers remain as si-trysts, seed- or choose-fathers are the most important people in a child's life. What sett were you raised in?'

The rill banks had narrowed, and the riders strung out in single file. Ithreya rode with Drasen just in front and Viv lowered her voice. 'I wasn't raised in a sett.'

'So, you were raised in one of the more remote cloudwise vals by your mother?'

'I was raised by my mother and choose-father until I was ten when my mother disappeared. Once she had gone, my choose-father moved us around. When I was fourteen, I left and lived with various other people. When I was eighteen, I met my seed-father for the first time, and he told me there was a way to find my mother, and I set out to find her.'

Viv took a steadying breath. Her throat had not narrowed which meant her angelic part had not judged her little speech to be untrue, but her human part was less easily fooled by her verbal sleights of hand. Her inability to lie had been more than an inconvenience growing up and her only recourse had been to stay silent, which had been seen as deceit, or worse, as a challenge.

'Fara sends images that suggest you experienced no love from either of your fathers,' said Sehereden. Viv had never seen Sehereden angry, even when Drasen had goaded him over the arsehole, but he was angry now.

'Fara's correct,' said Viv, and wondered what images the horse had conjured. Dung? A bucket of vomit?

'I know little of the Astraali, but it's incomprehensible to me your choose-father failed to treasure you.'

The notion of Jimmy Wright *treasuring* her was so ludicrous that Viv laughed. 'Both my choose- and seed-fathers were arseholes,' she said. 'Guess I was just unlucky.' Sehereden said nothing but Fara's ears flicked and Viv struggled to replace the memories of Jimmy Wright's violence, and Kald's callousness, with happier ones.

'You said you met your seed-father,' said Sehereden, after a little. 'Have you been to the Astraali city?'

'No,' said Viv, cursing herself for having opened a can of worms.

'Then your Astraali seed-father visited your val?'

'My seed-father visited me.'

'In your val?'

Viv could think of nothing to say that was not a lie and she could not tell Sehereden the truth. Silence stretched as she struggled to dredge up thoughts to trick Fara into sending Sehereden a useful response.

'Fariye told me you denied being Valen *or* Astraali, and when I asked about your parentage earlier, you refused to answer. You're not answering me now either, and yet it seems like a small thing. As an elddra living outside Astraal, you *must* have lived in a val, and your seed-father *must* have left Astraal to visit you. Are you protecting your mother? Is that it? Did she keep her Astraali liaison a secret?'

'My mother has nothing to be ashamed of,' said Viv angrily. 'She just had the misfortune to fall in love with an arsehole!'

'I'm not suggesting shame, Viv, I'm just trying to make sense of what you've told me. *If* you've met your seed-father, he must have come to the vals or you must have gone to the Astraali city.'

Viv's heart thudded as Sehereden directed Fara from the line of riders to a grove of trees. The rest of the group passed by with only cursory glances, probably thinking one or both needed to relieve themselves but Viv jumped from Fara's back and, by the time Sehereden had joined her on the ground, she had dumped her pack, undone her jacket, and was several lengths away.

'I'd never hurt you, Viv,' he said gently.

'You and your other half already have!'

'I can't undo the past and at times I've sensed you've forgiven me for it, if not my lein. I've sensed your heart is open to love too, perhaps even craves it, but to have a future together, you must tell me the truth.'

'We're not going to have a future together!'

'Your love for Fariye is strong. I don't believe you'll walk away from her, and your feelings for me could grow—if you allowed it. But love needs trust, and trust must have the truth.'

12

'Okay, so let's have the truth. We'll start with a little quiz. In a choice between me and your lein, who would you choose?'

Sehereden frowned. 'Leins have nothing to do with couplings.'

'They do in this case.'

'Are you saying you won't take me because of my lein?'

Viv hesitated, surprised that the answer was not as clear-cut as she had thought. 'He hates me and the feeling's mutual. It would make it hard to live in his sett, even *if* he allowed it, which he won't.'

'Time will heal such feelings but none of this answers my questions. Trust me, Viv. Tell me the truth.'

Viv dried her sweaty palms on her trousers. She knew nothing of how outsiders were treated here, apart from the elddra, and they were barely tolerated. And seared into her brain were the images of women, condemned as witches, and dragged to the flames. Sehereden's face was as tender as Rim's in their most intimate moments, and Viv took a shaky breath. 'I've said before that I don't lie. The truth is that I *can't* lie. Everything I've told you, Fariye, and to everyone else for that matter, is the truth, but I can't tell you everything. You have to understand that.'

Sehereden nodded and Viv sucked in more air. 'The truth is my choose-father beat my mother and after she disappeared, he beat me. When I was fourteen, his friend tried to rape me, and I left and lived the best I could on my own, scrounging food and shelter. I wasn't good at it and after a while I found other people who'd been like me, but who'd learned to fight and steal. Most put poisons in their bodies to make their lives bearable. I lived as they did. I thieved and traded sex to survive until I was caught and locked up.

'When my choose-father died, they let me out for his funeral. I met my seed-father there and he took me to where he lived. In his own way, he's as violent as my choose-father, but he gave me a guide to find my mother. My guide's name is Thrisdane. Our search has been difficult, and we've been separated more than once. The last time was when I found Fariye. You know most of what has happened since.'

'Fariye thinks Thrisdane's your lein-tryst. Is he?'

'No,' said Viv, but her throat tightened, and she dropped her head. She heard Sehereden's soft tread but raising her face was impossible, even when his arms came around her. The bald summary of her life had jarred her, and it took time for his warmth to ease her breathing.

He smelled of Fara and of the leather he wore, and of himself, not sweet like an angel, but still attractive. He kissed the top of her head, as he might a child's, but he did not speak, and Viv was grateful. His embrace told her he had accepted her words and though there might be more questions later, for now, it was enough.

Chapter 2

Sehereden quickened Fara's pace to catch the rest of the party but they rode in silence until a brief break at dusk. Viv made no attempt to hide her feelings, despite knowing Fara sent them to Sehereden. It had been a relief to open-up after months of guarding her every word, and if it turned out to be a mistake, she would be gone soon anyway.

Sehereden stayed close to her and his attention remained on her even when Drasen and Ithreya joined them at the rill. Viv might have felt uncomfortable but he launched into humorous descriptions of his less successful ridge descents. Viv had seen how Valen horses jumped down the ridges, but Sehereden made his misadventures so funny she laughed with the others.

'Ridge jumps are perilous,' said Ithreya softly, as soon as Sehereden and Drasen went to reclaim their mounts. 'If horse or rider make a mistake, there's no second chance. Some say Sehereden's leinship keeps him safe, that Enda favours Ataghan and those he loves.' Ithreya glanced sideways at her. 'It's said Ataghan once rode the Eshacade's floodwaters down from the Argine, using only his strength to stay afloat, and that, thanks to Enda's grace, his daughter survived when others perished, but of course you had a hand in it too.'

'I had nothing to do with her escape.'

'But a lot to do with keeping her safe afterwards. Sehereden's love for Fariye is strong and should Enda's benevolence desert Ataghan, he will become her choose-father.' Ithreya glanced in the direction the men had gone. 'Fariye's love for you adds to your desirability, of course, as does your beauty and while Sehereden's want of you is no surprise, I'm puzzled why you've changed your mind about *him.'*

'I'm not sure I have.'

'I am,' said Ithreya, with a tight smile. 'I admit I was relieved at the sett when you said you didn't want him, for no woman can compete with an elddra.'

'Valen men take many lovers,' said Viv with a shrug.

'Not once they are lein-trysted, and that's what I want with Sehereden, what I've wanted since I first saw him at Esh-accom five zadicans ago.'

Sehereden and Drasen were on their way back and Ithreya's speech quickened. 'When Sehereden came to Amethen's sett and atunement came early, I thought Enda had smiled on me, but Sehereden won't lein-tryst with *anyone* while he thinks he has a chance with you.'

Viv expected there to be more wrestling practise after the meal that night but the men produced instruments and began to play. There were yu's like Sehereden's, breathy flutes, and tiny bells shaken in time to the beat of palm-sized drums. Sehereden had told her earlier that travellers held their own festivities before they entered Esh-accom, for once within its walls, they were bound by its laws and customs, not their own.

The yu's reminded Viv of the Scharii but also of happier times with her mother who had played Irish music in the car as they headed into the Ranges. Lettie had told her tales of grandma Iris, great grandma Vacia, and great, great grandma Rose too. 'Copper-curled all of them, but not as lovely as you,' her mother had said.

16

'Or you,' Viv had replied as she had snuggled close.

She had loved the sense of being part of the mysterious Rose, Vacia, and Iris, but they had lived and died in Ireland and the USA, places as remote as the moon, unlike those of Amethen's sett who lived together and played tunes in perfect harmony, and even Sehereden, who was from a different sett, did not miss a beat.

The music ended, except for the drummers, and then the men danced, their gripped hands held high, their heads thrown back in a celebration of male potency that even Nurana's stout lein-tryst shared.

Viv's gaze went unwillingly to Sehereden, to his broad shoulders and narrow hips, and to his profile, achingly like Rim's. Ithreya wanted him permanently and exclusively, and Viv could understand why but it was not just his looks, for Rim had been handsome, it was his kindness, something Viv had not experienced in a man before. He had stayed the arsehole's knife, shown compassion after the rape, and fought to keep her alive since.

The music ended and Sehereden came to a stop in front of her. 'Dance with me, Viv,' he said, and held out his hand.

A new tune had started and Nurana and her lein-tryst already danced, surprisingly nimble given their age and the rough ground, but the dance was intricate. 'I don't know the steps,' said Viv.

'I'll teach you.'

Viv was aware of Ithreya's stillness and of Drasen loitering nearby. 'I'm sure Ithreya would like to dance,' she muttered.

'And *would* Ithreya like to dance?' asked Sehereden smoothly, turning to her.

'Indeed, I would,' she said and rose.

Drasen settled in the empty space beside her but Viv kept her attention on the dancers. Nurana and her lein-tryst danced with the ease of a couple long familiar with each other, but Sehereden and Ithreya danced like lovers, and a burn started deep inside Viv. She had never known the difference between jealousy and envy, except one meant you wished the other person harm and the other that you wished them well, and she wished Ithreya only the best.

'There'll be plenty of dancing in Esh-accom,' said Drasen. 'Fariye will teach you the steps.'

'I'm not staying in Esh-accom,' said Viv, her gaze on Sehereden and Ithreya's entwined bodies.

'It's best you do. It's the safest place at the moment. There's still time before Fire Zadic for Waradi and Ascadi filth to murder more of us and get home in time for their own festivities. Besides, I've heard you search for your mother and Esh-accom would be a good place to look. It triples in size during Fire Zadic as most setts send someone. If your mother's living in one of the vals, someone in Esh-accom is sure to know. What does she look like?'

'Like me.'

'She'll be easy to spot then. There won't be many women there as lovely as you.'

Viv knew she was rude to not acknowledge the compliment, but the dance had finished and Sehereden led Ithreya away towards the trees. 'Aren't the men of Amethen's sett annoyed Ithreya's gone off with an outsider?' she asked.

'It's still Cascade Zadic but if Enda smiles on Ithreya and a child is seeded, he smiles on us all.'

'But don't you resent her being with *Sehereden*?' pursued Viv.

Drasen frowned. 'Sehereden en-Scinta-ril places highly in the tournaments and is lein to a powerful Syld. Why would there be resentment?' Viv said nothing and Drasen paused. 'Of course, for all his qualities, Sehereden en-Scinta-ril isn't the only man worthy of a woman's consideration.'

Men waited near the fire and when Viv still said nothing, Drasen rose. 'Time to set the guards. I trust there'll be a chance to speak further in Esh-accom and to share at least one dance?'

Viv dredged up a smile and nodded. Drasen's company was preferable to the arsehole's and a large settlement would have others who shared the arsehole and Scharii's hatred of elddra too, who might corner her in some dark alley, as she had been cornered before. The possibility provided more reason not to hang about but what Drasen said also made sense. Her mother might even be in Esh-accom, as a visitor or inhabitant, especially if she had lein-trysted.

If only she could fly there now! Frustration boiled and she scrambled up and strode away into the trees, careful to choose the opposite direction to Sehereden and Ithreya, then climbed the first large tree she saw. Esh-accom's lights might be visible in the distance but then she reminded herself that settlements here were not like the cities back home and the darkness remained impenetrable.

She rested back against the bole and then the Cascade Zadic ignited, waking memories of her joining with Thris. God how she longed for his sweet touch, for the feel of his wings meshed with hers, for the ecstatic star-storm that made her complete. Viv's back burned as her wings fought to escape, and she gasped, overwhelmed by her want of him.

She needed to harmonise, or at least attempt to, and she started her climb down, but her head was so full of radiance she missed her footing, and half fell the last of the way, crying out as she drove a splinter deep into her palm.

'Viv! You've hurt yourself. Show me.' It was Sehereden, but she turned away, fighting to control her emotions. 'Show me,' he insisted. Viv kept her head down as Sehereden examined her hand. 'Is this your only injury?' Her angel part did not differentiate between old and new injuries and she could not answer. 'Viv?'

His voice was as gentle as his face, and hungry for comfort, she reached for him. He had just come from Ithreya but she needed the safety of his arms and the feel of his mouth on hers. The kiss was long and deep, and Viv gave herself up to it, not opening her eyes until Sehereden drew back.

It was a request to extend the kiss to something more and Viv was tempted to lose herself in love-making but had no stomach for the complications that would follow and she stepped back too. If he were disappointed, he did not show it. 'We'll see to that splinter,' he said, and led the way to the fire. It was quiet, those in their maarks already asleep, the guards nowhere to be seen.

'I've got atz somewhere to dull the pain,' he said, as he trawled in his pack.

'Just use your knife,' said Viv, wanting the whole episode over with.

'It will hurt.'

'I know,' she said, and gritted her teeth as the blade sliced along her palm. He was skilful, which was no surprise given knives were the weapon of choice, and deftly flicked the splinter out and poured water over the wound.

'I'll bind it for you.'

'No.'

'Elddra don't heal *that* quickly,' he said lightly.

'Nor do they suffer as the Valen do,' she said bitterly, repeating the arsehole's words before he shackled her to the urrut.

Sehereden obviously remembered them too. 'I don't believe my lein really thought that.'

'That's because you love him.'

'The love between leins is unalterable but not blind. When Ataghan believed himself robbed of Fariye, despair robbed him of other things too.'

'Like his sanity?' sneered Viv.

'Yes, for a time.' Orange sparks swirled as the fire coals collapsed but Sehereden's gaze did not waver, even when an owl swooped overhead. Viv watched it, glad of the diversion. 'A geist-owl,' said Sehereden, and drew an owl-shaped charm from his pocket. 'A gift for you.'

'Why?' asked Viv, making no move to take it.

'Because I know you like owls and I thought it would give you pleasure. Does it?'

'It is beautiful.'

'Good,' he said and clipping it to a fine chain, slipped it over her head. His face held the same intensity as earlier and while Viv no longer needed comfort, she did not want the moment to end either. His human maleness was different to Thris's angelic perfection, but it quickened her blood in the same way. The taste of him lingered from the last kiss and she drew him close, but his kisses were teasing now rather than passionate.

He let her choose the extent of their love-making, she realised, and that made him easy to want. She slid her hands under his shirt, enjoying the hardness of male muscle, but Sehereden made no attempt to caress *her*, and Viv wondered whether her love-making marked her as alien.

'Do you want somewhere more private?' he murmured when she hesitated. Sehereden offered her sex but Viv did not want to be another mark on his score card, but nor did she want the loneliness of lying sleepless in her maark. Sehereden smoothed back her hair. 'What is it you want, Viv?'

'I don't want ...' Shit. She did not even know what sex was called here. *Coupling*? Was that the term she had heard? 'I don't want *somewhere private,* but I don't want to be alone.'

'Easily solved,' he said. 'You can share my maark and that's all I'm asking you to share. I've been told I don't snore,' he added with a smile.

Chapter 3

Sehereden held the flap open and she ducked inside and sat as far from him as the sides allowed. There was enough light to see him take off his jacket and shirt, then his boots and slide under the cover. 'Aren't you going to lie down?' he asked.

'Perhaps I should go back to my own maark,' she said, aware that in the popular media's terms, she was *asking for it.*

Sehereden propped on his elbow. 'Do you think I'm going to attack you?'

'It's possible.'

'I can understand why you might believe that, given what you've told me,' he said. 'But you must have known men worthy of trust. What of your guide, Thrisdane? He's not been violent, has he?'

Sehereden's eyes bored into hers and she looked away. 'It wasn't his fault,' she muttered.

'Of course, it was his fault!'

Sehereden was no longer lying down and Viv felt like one of those women with blacked eyes and split lips who defended the violent bastards they loved, but nothing about Thris was simple. The pernicious influence of her father; Thris's yearning for ascendance; his bond with Ky; Moth Fold's corrosive effects on his sweet fibre and his protection of her in the cat creature's fold, all muddied the waters when it came time to judging him. And there was the exquisite joining of her angelic elements with his, sating her every need and waking a thousand more.

'Do you love him?' asked Sehereden more quietly.

'Yes.'

23

'Does he love you?'

There was a long silence. 'Maybe in some sort of way.'

'Is he elddric?'

'Elddric?' repeated Viv in confusion.

'The male of what you are. All things that couple birth males as well as females, *if* their line is to continue, so it follows there are elddric, even if the Valen are unaware of them.'

Sehereden was right, except male daimon were sterile, except they were not, she realised as she considered the Du-Daimon, off-spring of the Astraali, off-spring of the Angellus. She resembled the Iahhel and the elddra here must resemble them too, given she was mistaken for elddra, but the elddric obviously looked the same as everyone else. Lucky them, she thought acidly.'

'You haven't answered my question,' said Sehereden and Viv's attention jerked back to him.

'He's not elddric,' she said.

'And the love he has for you?'

'It's not what you think. It's just that he loves something else more,' she said and faltered as the truth of her words slammed home. Shit! She had known transcendence meant *everything* to him but in some dumb, romantic part of her brain, she had believed she would trump it, and even if she did, Thris would be condemned to Danehood long after her shorter daimon lifespan ended.

Viv sleeved her eyes. What a bloody idiot she had been and if Thris flapped down into the campsite now, she would be a bloody idiot all over again. Sehereden made no move to comfort her, just waited until she had her emotions under control.

'You've told me you're more likely to sleep after being hurt,' he said, as if they had just finished discussing the weather. 'Does your hand still pain you?' Viv shook her head but he crouched beside her and his warm fingers examined the wound. The cut's edges had already sealed, and he kissed it. 'Sleep, Viv,' he said, but his touch had reignited her need of him and she pulled him close.

'This is not a good time for you, Viv,' he said gently, and turned his face aside. 'It's best you sleep.'

'Best for *you*, perhaps,' she said and scrambled from the maark. Her exit coincided with the changing of the guard which meant soon the entire party would know her elddra scent had snared the lein of the mighty Syld Ataghan en-arsehole.

She headed uphill to where the trees were thicker, needing time alone. She had never dealt with rejection well and she had not needed the jail's shrink to know she could thank the loveless Jimmy Wright for it. Maybe it actually had nothing to do with Jimmy Wright, she thought sourly, as she scrambled upslope. Maybe she had inherited it from her mother after Kald had dumped her.

Viv knew Sehereden was being protective, but if she'd had her pack, she would have left, in fact, she still might. The zadic had faded and the chances of anyone noticing a large bird flapping away were small. She could say goodbye to Poss and be long gone before Sehereden's party arrived.

Good plan Vivi, except ya have no idea where the kid is. She could search, she countered, then imagined creeping along streets to peer into windows. And then there was her mother. She had to make sure Lettie was not in Esh-accom or nearby, or in the Astraali city before she quit this fold for good.

It would be sensible to stay with Sehereden but she feared she would be too weak to leave once they reached

Esh-accom. Sehereden offered her a place to call home and the fact that he was handsome, sensitive, and caring, meant she was in danger of being well and truly suckered.

The wind stirred, bringing the smell of smoke, then a twig snapped, and Viv had a split second to consider Sehereden probably still wrestled on his boots, when a hand clamped over her mouth and an arm became a choking bar across her throat. Viv clawed at the hand as she was hauled away upslope and the smell of smoke grew as she was dragged through a dense stand of bushes into the deeper darkness of a crevice.

Whoever had her shoved her hard in the back, and by the time she had regained her balance and turned, he had stamped out the fire, and his dim outline blocked any chance of escape. 'We've both made bad choices,' he said. 'Me lighting a fire and you taking a night-time stroll. How far is your camp?'

'It's near the rill,' she said, rubbing her neck.

'Is anyone likely to come looking for you?'

'Yes.'

'How soon?'

'He's probably looking now.'

The man cursed under his breath. 'I mean you no harm,' he said roughly. 'Who are you travelling with?'

'A party from Amethen's sett and Sehereden en-Scinta-ril.'

The man's head jerked round. 'Lein of the Syld, Ataghan en-Scinta-ril?'

'Yes,' said Viv, hoping to God her captor was not one of the arsehole's many enemies.

'Is Sehereden the man looking for you?'

'Probably.'

'I really have annoyed Soaich,' the man muttered. 'Of course, you could be lying.'

'I don't lie.'

He peered at her more closely. 'Maybe not, but you're inclined to steal mugs, aren't you?' Viv gaped at him. 'And blow-up camps, but I've heard you've also got a soft spot for sap-suckers and sick children. Have you kept your half of the bargain?'

Viv's thoughts jerked back to the man in the cave. 'I'll pass on the message when I get to Esh-accom. It's where the Syld is.'

'And the rest?'

Viv said nothing and the man's tension eased. 'I thought my kinsman was a fool to trust you, but maybe he wasn't. I certainly *hope* he wasn't,' he added and yanked her close. 'I imagine you want the child you cared for to stay safe?' Viv nodded. 'Esh-accom's crowded, particularly during Fire Zadic. It would be easy for her to go missing, and she will, *if* you speak of our meeting. Do you understand me?'

'Yes.'

'I'm leaving now. You'll wait here until Sehereden en-Scinta-ril finds you or dawn comes. You can use your elddra imagination to explain your absence and if you're thinking of calling out the moment I leave, rest assured, I'll know.'

The man hefted on his pack and as soon as he had gone, Viv slumped against the wall and slid down it until she was hunched on the floor. Her neck was sore but that was not the main damage he had inflicted. Counselling had told her that each new attack triggered the horror of the old, but not how to deal with it.

She should high-tail it back to Sehereden but she remained huddled in the shadows even when she heard him call outside. The crevice was well-hidden, and she did not emerge until the light crept in and was almost back to the camp before he saw her. 'Viv,' he exclaimed in relief, then his eyes narrowed. 'You're bruised. Tell me what happened.'

'I can't tell you,' she said, forcing her feet forward.

'Can't or won't?'

'What difference does it make?'

He wrenched her around to face him. 'Someone's hurt you, which is bad enough, but hiding who did it risks us all.'

'I've made a bargain, Sehereden, there's no risk to others,' she said, and jerking herself free, ducked into her maark.

Sehereden had a lot to think about as he rode. Viv's assailant might have been an Eshadi living rough, or a Waradi or Ascadi fighter, separated from their band and Sehereden's jaw tightened as he considered the bargain Viv might have made. His lein believed Viv was in league with the Waradi, and that Sehereden's attraction to blue eyes blinded him to her treachery, but his lein did not know Viv as he did, or hoped he did.

She remained silent but the images Fara sent were so bleak he felt like *he* was under attack and when they stopped at the Mira Rill's and Eshacade's junction to take their midday meal, she strode off along the bank. He followed and when she finally swung back to him, stood as if she readied for fight. 'Don't waste your time on an elddra, Sehereden!'

'I've never considered you a waste of time.'

'You did last night.'

28

'You told me you had traded yourself for food and shelter and I *never* want you to feel you have to trade yourself again, but don't mistake me, Viv. Nothing would give me greater joy than you gifting yourself to me, and not just because of your elddra beauty but because you carry love in your heart. When trust is built, when you're happy and settled, then it will be time for us, *if* you choose.' He paused. 'Of course, I might have been mistaken last night, as men often are, and if you do want to couple, there's time enough now.'

Viv stared at him as if she weighed his words *and* him, and he appraised her too. Distance robbed him of the full power of her scent but the taste and feel of her were imprinted on his being. He had never wanted a woman like this before and yet he believed he had been right to refuse her last night.

He wanted more than Fire Zadic's transitory gifts where even if he seeded a child it might be given elsewhere. Ithreya might favour him, for he sensed her gifts were driven by more than early atunement, but he wanted what his father had enjoyed and despite Anfarena's claim Valen could not meet an elddra's needs, he believed he could make Viv happy.

Thrisdane's absence also gave him an advantage, as did his closeness to Fariye. Everything pointed to Viv's love for the child and if an elddra could love a Valen child, she could love him, especially if he and the child were in the same place.

Viv still regarded him, but the tension had gone from her body. 'You're not like the other men I've known, or maybe you're just a better actor,' she muttered.

'*Actor*?'

'Someone who pretends to be something they're not.'

29

'Do you think I'm pretending to care about you? To want you?' he asked, angered despite himself.

Viv's answer was a long time coming. 'No. I think you're honest and true.' Sehereden knew how much the admission had cost her and that he had her trust now, and trust was the first step to love, a lein-tryst, and to raising their children together at the Scinta Rill.

Chapter 4

Ataghan propped Fariye on his hip as he stood atop Esh-accom's wall and stared cloudwise up the Eshacade's broad valley. It had become a ritual to come down to the wall each evening, watch the sun ebb nightwise beyond the forests, and see the lamps begin their twinkle in the buildings behind them.

They would eat their evening meal and then set out down the shady streets, through the drift of cooking smells, past the stables and across the open cobblestones in the wall's lee, then up the narrow steps to the walkway on top.

He held Fariye so she could see over the parapets, and they would watch the riders, and occasional wagon, make their way to Esh-accom's gate. Fariye was excited by what the wagons might hold, for traders brought all manner of exotic things to Esh-accom's festivities, but she was mainly excited by the prospect of her lein's return.

They would turn for home when the first stars glinted, Fariye's small hand in his, her chatter silenced by disappointment. Ataghan had tried to prepare her for the solitary return of *his* lein, but she would have none of it. *Ser will bring Viv back,* she insisted, but Ataghan knew Sehereden would wisely leave the elddra out of Fariye's sight, and hopefully, eventually out of her mind.

At best, the elddra's scarring would make her an object of curiosity, but there were setts in the more obscure rills where even red-haired children were slaughtered, so great was their fear of difference. He tightened his arms around Fariye as he considered the slaughter of his own sett and she suddenly twisted in his arms. 'They're coming!' she squealed.

There were riders on the track but dusk purpled the air and even his keen eyes could not tell whether Fara was amongst them. 'It's them! It's them!' she insisted shrilly, drawing the glances of others. There were more people on the wall than usual, despite the closeness of Vorash, for as the festivities neared, Esh-accom's citizens became increasingly curious about the wares soon to be offered.

Metal-wrights did a roaring trade with the tribute-charms men gave to encourage and celebrate women's *gifts*, as did those who demanded coin to reveal cages that contained everything from two-headed urrut calves to cowed and dirty Lefer who bore the marks of whips. Ataghan had no appetite for such things but Esh-accom's Sylds were a lot keener on the smooth flow of trader-tributes than on the welfare of creatures from The Wheel's more distant vals.

Fariye continued to squeal and more people mounted the wall to discover the cause of her excitement. The riders were close enough now to see that some horses carried two. Women owned and rode horses but often rode behind their leins when they journeyed together.

The last of the light glanced off the fair hair of one of these women and then Fara emerged from the throng and Ataghan saw that he carried two as well. 'Ser's got Viv! Ser's got my lein!' shrieked Fariye, squirmed from his arms and sped off down the steps.

People smiled indulgently but Ataghan's knuckles whitened on the parapet. What in Enda's name had possessed Sehereden to bring the elddra back? The top of the elddra's head passed out of sight under the wall and he turned in time to see the elddra throw herself from Fara's back as Fariye sprinted to meet her.

Ataghan was barely aware of the scatter of applause from on-lookers as Fariye leapt into the elddra's arms, his attention taken by the elddra's *unmarked* face, filled with relief, as she held Fariye close.

He took the steps two at the time to dispel the heat that burned him and the crowd parted to let him through. Up close the blonde-haired woman was beautiful, with the blue eyes his lein admired, but Sehereden's gaze was on the elddra.

Then his lein saw him and they embraced. 'It's good to be back,' said Sehereden.

Sehereden's touch quenched the fire in his flesh, as it always did. 'It's good to *have* you back,' he replied. Even without the threat of attack, the journey to Tahsin's sett was dangerous and, despite Sehereden's denials, Fara was far from the agilest horse in the band.

'This is Ithreya en-Verra-ril, of Amethen's sett,' said Sehereden, introducing the fair-haired woman. 'The rest of the party is of Amethen's sett too.'

Ataghan had no idea why Sehereden had diverted to the Verra-ril but there would be time to discuss that later *and* why he had brought the elddra back. His lein's gaze had returned to her but she still held Fariye, their foreheads close as they exchanged words too low to hear, and Ataghan turned to Ithreya. 'You've had a pleasant journey?'

'Mostly,' she said, her eyes flicking to Sehereden. 'Viv was attacked last night.'

'By whom?' demanded Ataghan.

'She won't say,' said Sehereden.

'In which case, she might be glad of your *female* company here, Ithreya,' said Ataghan smoothly. 'My compound has many empty rooms and is convenient to the wrights. If you would like to join us, I can beg permission from whomever represents your sett.'

'I'm sure Drasen will have no objections,' said Ithreya quickly.

'I'll request it on your behalf, as I'm known to him,' said Sehereden. Ataghan's eyes narrowed as he watched Sehereden thread his way through the crowd and Ithreya hurry after him and slide her arm through his.

The elddra had set Fariye down and his daughter now pulled her excitedly towards him. When Ataghan had left her at Tahsin's sett, her face had been a rucked mask, and while it was not now, it was not as he remembered it. She had been half mad with terror after he had dispatched her stinking Waradi comrades, but still defiant, as she was now. But she had benefitted from her time with Tahsin and the combination of dark red curls, fair skin, and deep blue eyes, was so striking that those in the yard stared.

'Welcome to Esh-accom,' he said formally.

'It's bigger than I expected,' she said, staring at the buildings to avoid acknowledging him.

'It has lots of wrights,' said Fariye excitedly. 'We can show Viv around tomorrow, can't we, da? I want to visit the shallit stalls and we must get a casque. Viv hasn't got a casque for her amé, da, and I know where the good ones are. Ser showed me while you were away. And after that we can go all the way around the wall, like we did after you came back, and then—'

Ataghan raised his hand. 'First things first, Fariye. Your lein's been riding all day and might want to rest and eat. We'll decide later what's to be done on the morrow.'

'She can sleep in my room, can't she, da?' asked Fariye, grabbing his hand. She still held the elddra's and Ataghan caught the elddra's scent as Fariye's small body

34

tugged them closer. The scent stirred memories of the killing when she had carried the Waradi's scent too and hatred for the Waradi burned anew.

'There are plenty of rooms, Fariye,' he said.

'Then next to my room. Can she, da? Can she?'

'We'll see.'

Poss kept up a stream of chatter as they followed the arsehole through the streets and, despite the arsehole's presence, all Viv felt was relief. Poss skipped along beside her like a normal little girl, happy and safe.

The streets grew less crowded as they moved away from the wall but there were still more people than Viv had seen in her entire time in the fold. Esh-accom reminded her of a film set of medieval England with double-storeyed wooden buildings squeezed along the sides of stone-paved streets, and splashes of lamp light escaping from shuttered windows. The food smells were the same as Tahsin's sett and she felt a pang of longing. She even missed Enesha's surliness and tightened her grip on Poss's hand.

Poss squeezed back. 'There's lots of cloth-wrights here,' she said, pointing at the shuttered stalls. Wooden plaques were fixed near the doors painted with variations on scissors, rulers, thread, and needles, and Viv noticed buildings with plaques showing bowls and spoons. Not all their shutters were closed, and she glimpsed crowds of diners.

The arsehole led them on, turning here and there, and the dimness added to Viv's disorientation. People jostled each other where the streets narrowed, but no one jostled the arsehole, probably because he was a *Syld*, whatever that was.

35

She still had to honour the deal she had made with the man in the cave and the thug who had half strangled her last night had been keen the message be delivered too. Viv had not wasted time trying to work out who the men were beyond the fact they were not the Eshadi's enemies. The second man had known the first, and the first man had aided an Eshadi child. Viv had no idea what the war was about either but if it were anything like the wars at home, it would be over land, resources or religion, or even racial *purity* given her *welcome*.

The streets grew quieter and the stalls and buildings gave way to high stone walls with lush-looking trees visible above. The wealthy always lived in such quiet shady places, which had saved Viv time finding the best houses to rob. She even found herself searching the walls for toeholds.

The arsehole pushed open a heavy wooden gate, and they followed him into a courtyard. Stables ran along one side, the house along another, and a large tree with pale, highly-perfumed, waxy flowers took up the centre. Its petals strew the paving and might have been glis blooms except for the colour.

The house looked like Tahsin's sett except for the colonnaded veranda that ran along the front. Lamp light told her others were inside and she hoped to God they included Sehereden and Ithreya; she needed their kind faces to counteract the arsehole's.

'Does it have your approval, elddra?' the arsehole asked mockingly, and Viv glanced at Poss.

The little girl collected petals, but she was still within earshot, and Viv swallowed her retort. 'Who leads the Sylds?' she asked instead.

'No one,' he said in surprise. 'Why do you ask?'

'I have a message for their leader but if there isn't one, you'll do.' She paused and then said clearly, *Enda lies nightwise.*'

'Who told you to say that?' he hissed.

'A man I made a bargain with to keep me and Poss alive,' said Viv softly, aware of Poss's proximity.

The arsehole caught her arm and dragged her further away. 'And he was?'

'Part of the bargain was not to speak of him.'

'Let me guess then, elddra. He was the Waradi who gave you the mug and who you trysted with last night.'

'I keep my promises.'

'Which are to spy on me and those in Esh-accom!'

'I promised Fariye I wouldn't leave her without a proper farewell,' she said angrily, 'and that's another promise I'll keep! I'll do it now and be on my way.'

Poss's collection of petals scattered as she dashed back to Viv's side. 'No! You're my lein. You *have* to stay here. Da will let you stay, won't you, da? It's not Viv's fault her father's Astraali. It's not Viv's fault!'

Tears streamed down Poss's face and Viv hoisted her into her arms and held her close. 'I told you I was looking for my mother,' she said gently. 'I told you I wouldn't be able to stay.'

'No!' shrieked Poss, flinging her arms around Viv's neck and holding on tight.

The gate swung open and Sehereden appeared with Ithreya. 'What's this, Fari?' he asked, tweaking her plait. 'I thought we'd been invaded by asht-sprites, so loud is your wailing.'

'Viv's—Viv's leaving,' she sobbed.

'Not for many zadics, Fari. I happen to know she's promised Drasen a dance at the festivities, and she can't

37

dance with him until she's danced with me, *and* with you, and before that, you have to teach Viv *how* to dance and, although I'm sure Viv's a quick learner, there are so many dances, it will take ages for her to learn them all. And then,' he said, giving her plait another tweak, 'she'll have to wait until we rebuild the sett, because our sett was the most beautiful of all the setts and Viv can't possibly leave without seeing it as it was.

'By then it will be Ice Zadic and maybe even Lirium, and the esta will be in bloom and the erali, and the scinta-pool will be strewn with their petals, and it will be so lovely that Viv won't be able to bear to leave at all.' He brought his arms around them both, but his gaze was on Viv. 'And so, you see, there's nothing to be upset about at all.'

Poss was smiling through her tears but Viv was aware that the arsehole's gaze flicked between her and Sehereden. He was not going to be thrilled with his lein's interest, but he had nothing to worry about. There would soon be lots of women vying for Sehereden's attention, in addition to Ithreya, and even if Viv did find her mother and hung around, a despised elddra would be the last thing on his mind.

Chapter 5

The arsehole's compound reminded Viv of the Keeper's house in Hearth Fold, probably because they both smelled of fresh-baked bread, or retsen, as it was called here, but the arsehole's compound was far grander. The flag-stone floors were covered with patterned rugs, brass and copper ornaments gleamed in wall niches, and many doors opened off the passageway they went down. She assumed they were bedrooms and that meant many people shared the compound.

Poss perched on Viv's hip, her arms still tight around Viv's neck, and as the hum of voices grew ahead, Viv braced herself. A large table occupied the centre of the hall, which was usual but, unlike Tahsin and Amethen's setts, the kitchen was not hidden away behind doors, but sat against the far wall. Its fire warmed the room, and the smell of fresh bread strengthened.

About a dozen men stood about talking, but it was the table's wooden chairs that caught Viv's eye, their backs and arms beautifully carved with swirls of flowers, exotic birds, galloping horses, and what looked like stalactites and stalagmites in limestone caves.

'Da carved them,' murmured Poss, seeing her interest. 'He carved ones with Sita on them too, but they were at the Scinta-ril …'

Poss trailed off and Viv kissed the top of her head. 'I'm sure he'll carve some more when he and Sehereden rebuild your sett,' she said, surprised the arsehole was capable of anything but murder.

A grey-haired man appeared through a door near the kitchen with a haul of firewood and young woman hurried back and forth as she added platters of food to the table. 'Are you ready to eat, Syld?' she asked.

'Shortly, Mereya,' he said, shrugging out of his jacket.

The arsehole's muscular shoulders reminded her of Rim, as did the way he scanned the room. His expression did not change as his glance passed over her, but his black eyes were so full of animosity she doubted she would spend even a night there.

'Let's choose some rooms while we wait,' said Sehereden cheerfully, and taking up a lamp, headed back down the passageway. Viv and Ithreya followed, Poss still clinging to Viv like her possum namesake. 'Mereya will set some lamps now we're here,' he said over his shoulder.

'Does she live here too?' asked Viv.

'Mereya and her choose-father, Tormis, ready the compound for our arrival which is usually towards the end of Cascade. It's closed-up most of the zadican, but if we need to visit at other times, it doesn't take long to prepare. They live close by but sometimes stay here too.'

It's large for so few of you,' murmured Viv, thinking of Tahsin's sett.

'There were more of us before Esh-embrin,' said Sehereden. Viv was annoyed she had failed to work that out for herself and at Sehereden's brutal bluntness in front of Poss. 'Which is why those of us who care about Viv en-elddra, want her safely here with us,' he added conversationally.

'That's da's room,' piped Poss, pointing at a door, 'and that's mine, and that's Ser's. I'm between da and Ser, although da says nothing comes between leins,' she added and giggled as if it were a private joke. 'Share my room, Viv,' she said, wriggling down, and tugging at her hand. 'I'll show you how nice it is.'

Viv followed her in and stopped; it was more than nice, it was beautiful. The wooden bedhead was carved with flowers, by the arsehole no doubt, and the sumptuous quilt embroidered with horses.

'I had a quilt like this when I was a child,' said Ithreya with a smile, 'but mine had stars. My father traded it from a cloth-wright near the Old Quarter.'

'We can get one for Viv's bed,' said Fariye excitedly, pointing to a second bed pushed against the wall. 'And here's a present for my lein,' she added, dashing to it, and retrieving a cloth-bound bundle. She unwrapped it excitedly to reveal a tunic top and trousers in blue with patterning picked out in gold and silver thread. 'Do you like them, lein?' asked Poss. 'Ser said they should fit you.'

'They are lovely. Thank you,' said Viv. Poss might be too young to wonder how Sehereden knew her size *before* he had collected her but Ithreya's puzzled gaze told Viv she was not. 'You have so many beautiful things,' said Viv quickly, staring at the shelf above Poss's bed.

It was loaded with wooden dolls and enamelled models of urrut, horses, Lefers, and strange birds like heavily-crested peacocks. She stared at the Lefer as she recalled the kindness of the blue-crested one and the red-crested one's aggression.

'That's a parien,' said Poss, mistaking her interest for the peacock-like bird. 'They're not here anymore because the Angellus coupled with them to make the Lefer, and then the Angellus left. I've got a parien feather though,' she said, and took a carved wooden chest from the shelf, carefully removed a feather, and handed it to Viv. It looked like a pink and purple peacock feather.

'We don't know that *any* of these things are true,' cautioned Sehereden. 'The Lefer might have always been

41

here, like us, and the parien might still be here too, but hidden away.'

'But no one's seen any parien for zadicans, Ser, so my feather's special, isn't it? Da went beyond the Rimming to get it, didn't he?'

'I'm not sure. He might have traded it at the festivities.'

'I have another one for your collection,' said Viv, retrieving her feather from her pocket. 'I'm afraid it's not as colourful as the parien feather.'

'Oh, it's lovely,' cried Poss, 'and so silky.' She ran it over her face. 'And it smells of you!'

'It's been in my pocket,' said Viv brightly.

'What sort is it, Ser?' she asked, handing it to Sehereden. 'Ser knows *all* the birds,' she boasted.

'I have no idea,' said Sehereden, holding it up to the lamplight. 'Where did you find it, Viv?'

'At Tahsin's sett,' said Viv. 'Oh, what a nice view of the tree you have,' she said, going to the window.

'It's a magellus. Da brought the seed back from one of his trips and planted it there for me. It's the only magellus in the whole of Esh-accom.'

'That was nice of him,' said Viv, but she was not thinking of the arsehole, but of her attacker. The tree's cover made the yard an intruder's delight. 'Your room's so pretty I think I *will* share it,' she said.

Poss squealed in delight but Sehereden was far less pleased. 'Fariye needs to be abed early. It will make your coming and going difficult.'

'I'm a thief, remember. I'm *very* quiet.'

'You *were* a thief,' said Sehereden softly, coming to the window. 'But I promise you, Viv, you'll never have to steal what is rightfully yours again.'

Ithreya's face told Viv she had heard Sehereden's pledge but Poss was oblivious. 'It will be like when Ser and da share a maark,' she rushed on. 'Da and *his* lein sleeping together, and me and *my* lein sleeping together.'

'Now we must find an equally pretty room for Ithreya,' said Sehereden. They did not need to search far. The passageway was full of empty rooms and Ithreya chose the one opposite his.

Their return to the hall signalled the meal's start and the arsehole deftly directed the seating so that Sehereden and Ithreya were at the head of the table with him, and Viv was at the bottom with Poss and the less important men. He obviously intended it as a slight as well as conveniently separating her from his lein, but it suited Viv. Everyone's attention was on him, which left her free to reconnoitre in case she needed a quick getaway.

The kitchen door opened to the outside, given that Tormis had used it to deliver wood, as did the passageway door they had entered by. The rooms on the same side as Poss's faced the front yard like hers, and their windows provided exit points. If the compound followed the same layout as Tahsin and Amethen's setts, there would be an internal courtyard too, bounded by the building. All in all, the quickest way out was from Poss's window.

Some of the men who ate with the arsehole had massacred the Waradi and she had no doubt they remembered the *Waradi's lein-tryst* but they betrayed neither recognition *nor* animosity, and Viv did not know whether to be angry or relieved. Maybe the nearness of the *festivities* blinded them to all else!

She was in no mood to attempt polite conversation with them regardless but Poss did not give her the chance anyway, talking nonstop about something called shallit, the wagons that held all sorts of strange creatures, the cloth- and metal-wrights' pretty produce, the dances in Axian, the tournaments, and all the things she and Viv would do at the Scinta-ril.

Poss spoke as if they shared a future and Viv blamed Sehereden. He had painted a rosy picture of them all living together like one big happy family but even if Viv's search for her mother had not prevented it, the arsehole's hatred certainly would.

The table was loaded with food that included meatballs spiced with whatever she had smelled in the streets, vegetables like dark red and purple carrots, retsen disks, and cheese she presumed was made from urrut milk. The drinks were either water or urrut milk, the latter sprinkled with spice. There were no alcoholic drinks on the table, which meant the arsehole must smoke or snort whatever he was on.

Poss was yawning by the time the platters of fruit arrived, and Viv glanced towards the arsehole to see if he had noticed his daughter's weariness. He spoke with a grizzled man to his left but when he turned back to Sehereden on his right, deliberately avoided looking in her direction. Viv's lips thinned and she scooped up Poss and, without excusing herself or bidding anyone good night, strode from the room.

The passageway was now well lit and there was a lamp in Poss's room too. Viv deposited Poss on the bed and pulled off her boots while Poss struggled out of her clothes. 'What do you wear to sleep in?' asked Viv. Poss lifted her pillow to reveal a night dress, and Viv slipped it over her head. The material was soft and had blue daisies embroidered across the bodice.

'Da took me to the cloth-wrights this morning and let me choose two,' said Poss. 'The other one's got esta on it.'

The arsehole certainly loved his daughter, conceded Viv, and wondered how her life would have been like had *she* had the powerful protective love of a father. For one thing, the loss of her mother would not have meant the loss of everything. Her face must have betrayed her feelings because Poss suddenly pulled her close. 'You won't ever leave without saying a proper goodbye, will you, lein?'

'I'll never just disappear from your life, Poss,' she said fiercely. 'I promise.'

Chapter 6

Poss was soon asleep but Viv was too restless to even lie down. She wandered around the room, careful not to disturb Poss, knowing she must start her search of Esh-accom at first light. Easier said than done. Looking up the local phone book was not an option and even if she walked the streets, the chances of bumping into her mother were slim.

She took a deep breath and tried to think logically. Given the arsehole had his own compound, her mother might have too, *if* she lived here, and her colouring would also make her stand out. But if she did not live here and visited for the festivities, she would likely use the equivalent of a hotel. Viv guessed the buildings would have plaques to identify them, but if not, she would ask Sehereden where visitors stayed, or ask Ithreya, *if* Ithreya were still talking to her.

Viv stopped and stared into space. Esh-accom had reminded her why she was in the Rynth in the first place and her search meant she was no threat to Ithreya's happily-ever-after with Sehereden. And if her mother *did* live here …' Shit! Viv would have to live here too, in the same town as the arsehole.

Viv stifled a mirthless laugh. He did not live here *all* the time, Viv reminded herself, but for the first time in her thoroughly stuffed-up search, she hoped she would *not* find her mother in the fold she visited. But *if* she were here, living in Esh-accom, how did she support herself? And if she had partnered with a man to put a roof over her head, he sure as hell was not going to be thrilled by another man's daughter turning up and wanting the same.

There was no reason her mother *would* be here rather than some other fold, except the fold's symmetry had attracted angels, whose descendants still lived here, and her mother had got herself tangled up with angels before. Viv had not seen any other redheads but red hair was not common at home either.

The tournament finals would draw lots of people, as would the festivities, and it would be easy to spot any redheads then, but *then* was not now and Viv ground her teeth in frustration. If only this bloody night would end! She pushed the shutters wide and peered out. The Cascade Zadic had not even begun and she swung herself onto the window ledge. The drop was less than a body-length and she landed softly and paused in the colonnade's shadows. The arsehole and Sehereden's rooms were to either side, and still dark, which told her the dinner party was still in full swing.

The magellus loomed in the yard, its massive spreading branches dark, its blossoms pale blotches, and the shadowy faces of horses watched her from the stables. She was still confused by the whole horse-colour thing but the flick of their ears told her they communicated, she just hoped it was with each other and not their riders.

She expected to be challenged or the gate to be locked, but neither were the case and she slipped out into the street. Now what? Perhaps a bit of reconnaissance to save her time tomorrow. She set off, keeping to the shadows and ears straining for sound, turned left at the first juncture, and headed downhill as she recalled that Esh-accom's buildings *rose* behind the wall. The cobbled streets seemed like a collection of T-intersections and as she went, there were more people around, walking briskly as if only interested in reaching their homes. There was the

47

occasional wagon too, drawn by what looked like smaller versions of urrut.

She memorised the landmarks to aid her return but the only light there was seeped from partially opened shutters. She went on, always downhill and as she neared the wall gate, the grind of metal treads heralded more wagons, and she had to press close to a wall to let them pass. They were crudely painted, the second with what looked like a birdman, although it could have been the mysterious parien, given the garish colours.

She stared after them as she recalled the gaming ring, and then a man stepped from the shadows and continued down the street. Viv had not seen his face last time either, but she had no doubt it was the man who had attacked her, and that he had recognised her too.

Viv turned back the way she had come and broke into a jog. She had kept her side of the bargain, so Poss should be safe, but why was the man in Esh-accom? She glanced behind her often as she went but he had no need to follow to know where the arsehole lived; probably all of Esh-accom knew the address of the great Ataghan en-Scinta-ril.

She half-expected the gate to be locked, given how late it was, but it remained open and she closed it behind her and hastened across the yard. Poss's window-shutters were still wide too, but as she gripped the sill to swing herself up, she was seized and wrenched backwards. For a terrifying moment she thought the man *had* followed her but it was the arsehole.

He was angry, which was nothing new, and dragged her away from Poss's window to the tree. 'There are certain courtesies involved in living in my compound,' he hissed, releasing her with a savage shake. 'And they don't involve sneaking in and out of windows in the middle of the night.'

'But apparently *do* involve attacking your guest!'

'You'll never be that.'

Viv knew she should fling an insult back but the words stung. He was right, she would never be more than a barely tolerated intruder, and she could not remember a time when it had been different. Only Tahsin had ever welcomed her. The sky was still empty of the Cascade Zadic making it hard to see the arsehole's face, but she sensed he regretted his words. Maybe he had breached some sort of *Syld* code of honour, she thought sourly.

'You should set guards,' she said, rubbing her bruised arms.

'Why?' he demanded.

'Because it's a nasty, dangerous world, arsehole, and you need to keep your daughter safe.'

'Safe from whom? Your Waradi comrades?'

'Just do it,' she said, weary of the constant fighting.

She turned away, but he called her back. 'You'll use the door, this time, elddra.' His tone was sneering, and she headed along the colonnaded walkway in what she hoped was the right direction. It was, for she met some of his *guests* leaving. She kept her gaze on the stone floor but as she reached Poss's room, the door opposite opened and Sehereden came out. Ithreya's room, recalled Viv, which explained why he buttoned his shirt.

'Viv . . .' he began, but she slid into Poss's room and for a long time, simply stood with her head resting against the door. Poss's face was peaceful in sleep, her bed warm and clean, the room full of pretty things gifted by a man who loved her. Viv had fulfilled her pledge to reunite Poss with her family so there was no reason to linger, at least not here, where she was so unwelcome.

She removed the chain with its owl charm and slid it into her pocket with the Waradi tryst-bracelet. She had no idea how much each was worth, but Sehereden did not strike her as a cheapskate. The bracelet's Waradi decoration probably made it worthless as jewellery but its silver should buy her a few night's accommodation somewhere. She still felt loath to part with it, which was odd, given what it had cost her *and* the birdmen, and it had never been hers anyway. A thief until the end, she conceded dryly.

Fariye was her usual chirpy self at breakfast and her bubbliness, as she perched beside Viv, was infectious but Viv tensed each time she heard footsteps. It turned out to be either Tormis carting water or wood, or Mereya with more retsen, honey, and milk.

'Ataghan and Sehereden are practising for the tournaments,' said Ithreya, as if she guessed Viv's thoughts. 'They have their own rink. Sehereden showed me last night.'

Viv was tempted to ask what else Sehereden had shown her last night but kept the jibe to herself. *Jealousy rearin' its scaly green head, eh Vivi*? It was, but Sehereden was not her lover and she was about to quit the compound and at some point, the entire fold. Sehereden and Ithreya were a good match too, so why did she not feel happy for them? *Cos ya still want the fairy tale, Vivi*, Rim's voice sneered.

The door opened and the arsehole and Sehereden came in, obviously fresh from their practice. Both wore the loincloths the men had trained in at Amethen's sett, and the citrus-smelling oil that highlighted every ripple in their considerable muscles. They were of similar height but the arsehole was broader across the shoulders and carried himself as if under attack.

He sat opposite, close enough to Ithreya to touch her, but Ithreya looked anything but uncomfortable. The arsehole's gaze settled on Poss and his expression flashed to tenderness and then back to antipathy with such suddenness, Viv wondered if she had imagined it. Sehereden sat beside Poss, his gaze on Viv too, but *his* expression was playful. 'Guess who won our practice, Fari,' he said, reaching for retsen.

'Da!' she said gleefully.

'And who do you think will win the tournament?'

'Da!' she giggled and turned to Viv. 'Da always wins.'

'Not always,' said the arsehole, downing a mug of milk, and refilling it from the jug. Mereya delivered more retsen rounds, still steaming from the oven, and a bowl of cheese as soft as scrambled eggs.

'And what are your plans for the day, Fari?' asked Sehereden as he loaded his retsen with cheese.

'I want to take Viv to the metal-wrights to get her an amè casque. Look, Ser. She's only got an old bit of cloth to protect it,' and before Viv could stop her, Poss slid her fingers into Viv's open-necked shirt. 'You're not wearing it,' she said in shock, and Viv heard Ithreya's sharp intake of breath. 'You must *always* wear your amè, lein. Quick, go put it on.'

'I don't have it anymore, Poss.'

Poss's mouth formed a circle. 'Did the bad men take it?' she asked, with a catch in her voice.

'Yes,' said Viv, keeping her gaze on Poss.

'I . . . I know they hurt you, lein. Is that why you didn't come back straight away? Because you needed to heal?'

Shit! This was the last conversation she wanted to have with Poss, especially in front of the arsehole. 'Yes,' she said again.

'And are you healed now?' Lying was not an option and Viv trawled about for a way to fudge the truth. 'Are you, lein?'

'No.'

Poss crawled onto Viv's lap, brought her arms around Viv's neck, and held her close. It was as if only they two were present, as they had been at other awful times. Viv hugged her too as she struggled to come up with a light-hearted remark to break the tension, but her throat had closed over.

Then Sehereden's arms came around them both. 'There are wrights near the Old Quarter who have pretty amè casques, Fari,' he said softly. 'We can look there. The first step in replacing an amè, is to have a casque to keep it safe. But before that,' he added, with a smile, 'I must bathe. And *before* I can do that, Fari, I must have some of your *fortunate water*.'

Fariye scrambled from Viv's lap and took off down the passageway, Sehereden in mock pursuit, and Ithreya rose. 'I thank you for your hospitality, Syld,' she said. 'I must visit those of my sett, and my kin who have made their homes here.' The arsehole nodded and Ithreya turned to Viv. 'I've been to Esh-accom many times and it would be my pleasure to show you some of its more beautiful places.'

'Thank you, Ithreya. I'm probably leaving in the next few days, but if I'm still here, that would be lovely.' Ithreya looked surprised but nodded to Viv, and to the arsehole again, and disappeared down the passageway.

'Fariye's *fortunate water* is a game my lein's played with her since she was very small,' said the arsehole, before Viv could make her escape. 'Here it's strewing his bathing water with magellus blossoms, and at the Scinta Rill, with esta and erali petals. He tells her it makes him strong for the tournaments and, as he places well, it might be true.'

The arsehole actually sounded rational but the way he sprawled opposite, near-naked, his black eyes appraising her like a snake sized up a mouse, reminded her of Rim at his worst, and she slid from the bench. 'Stay,' he ordered. 'We need to speak of last night.'

'No, we don't. You made it clear I'm not welcome here so there's nothing to add *unless* you've thought up a new insult to add to the list.' He rose and Viv glanced about for an escape route. 'I only came here to say goodbye to Poss. I'll do that and find somewhere else to stay.'

'And use what as trade?' he asked contemptuously.

'I still have this,' said Viv and brandished the tryst-bracelet, 'and if that's not enough for a bed for a few nights, I'll toss in this,' she added and held up charm on its chain.

'Who gave you that?'

'Obviously a Valen I snared with my elddra scent.' His gaze was hard, but she saw how he sifted the possibilities. It would not take much wit to guess it was his lein, given she had the tryst-bracelet back, but she had a feeling the leinship prevented him asking outright.

'You'd be unwise to reveal you own a Waradi tryst-bracelet, elddra. Many here have lost family to Waradi knives and even your skin's *perfume* won't be enough to save it. As for the tribute-charm, it would insult the giver to trade it.'

'As I need somewhere to stay, arsehole. I don't have the luxury of *not* insulting people.'

'You do. You can remain here.' Viv blinked. Whatever he had snorted before their altercation last night had obviously worn off. 'You're my daughter's lein and, as such, her guest.'

'I was *her* guest last night.'

'It slipped my mind,' he said, and strode from the room.

Chapter 7

They were not far into their exploration of Esh-accom that morning before Viv revised her opinion of Sehereden as being caring and kind-hearted, having to add charming, amusing, *and* attentive as well. God only knew how he put up with the arsehole. Poss skipped along holding Viv's hand, and Sehereden walked on her other side, so close his body brushed hers in a way that was far from accidental.

He was clean-shaven, his hair glossy in the sun; his shirt, jacket, and close-fitting trousers black, with the cuffs patterned in blue. It was the same patterning as on her and Poss's clothes, and in the caves, but subtly different to the tryst-bracelet, which told her each Vale had its own design.

Viv had disliked being dirty and ragged in the vals but it would have been many times worse here and she mentally thanked Ithreya for her gift of clean, undamaged, and prettily-coloured clothes. The air's fragrance told her there were gardens with flowering shrubs behind the walls they passed but Sehereden said that many of the compounds were empty outside of Fire, Lirium, and Glimwing Zadics.

Viv nodded but had no idea why Lirium and Glimwing Zadics should be special. Maybe there was a second and third round of tournaments and festivities, although given the build-up to Fire Zadic's, it seemed unlikely. 'The sun's nice,' she said, as they emerged from the shade into more open streets.

'Best enjoy it while you can,' said Sehereden. 'It will rain later.' The sky was cloudless and Viv's surprise must have shown. 'Remember we're in Vorash.'

Viv wondered what sort of constellation Vorash was and given she had seen none over the previous few days, it might be brief like the owl one and she had missed it. Sehereden's keen eyes were on her, obviously noting her confusion, and she cursed her lack of care. It was easy to relax in his company and to forget she was an alien, in an alien fold.

'Can we get some shallit, Ser?' asked Poss.

'Shallit's a treat, Fari, not for every day.' Poss's disappointment was clear but she did not complain, and Sehereden's mouth kinked. 'Of course, we can get some for Viv, because she hasn't had any yet, and I'm sure she'll share with her lein, as leins always do.'

Poss turned to Viv excitedly. 'What sort do you like best, Viv?'

'I don't know, Poss. They don't have it where I'm from.'

'But everywhere has shallit.'

'You'll have to show me all the different sorts and help me choose,' said Viv, avoiding looking at Sehereden.

The confectioners turned out to be popular, with a queue eager to sample its wares, and Sehereden handed Fariye traders and settled on a bench to wait. He watched Viv perch Fariye on her hip and heads swivelled as she joined the line. Viv smiled as Fariye pointed at the shallit samples on display and then laugh as Fariye whispered something in her ear.

Sehereden had only seen Viv laugh twice before, once when he had concocted a comical tale of his ridge-crossings, and once with derision, when he had suggested her choose-father should have loved her. He wanted to see that laugh more often and his determination hardened to have her happily settled with him as a lein-tryst.

And yet, there was so much about her that made no sense and that one way or another, she refused to explain. Growing in an obscure rill might have made her ignorant of shallit but not of Vorash, and while she had offered herself to him on the journey here, she had been distant since. He did not want the trust he had managed to build to slip away, and he wondered whether Ithreya's presence was the problem or his lein's.

Women welcomed the attention of many suitors at Fire Zadic, and men competed to have their tribute-charms accepted and, in the end, themselves, for only then were children possible. Ithreya would gift herself to other men during the festivities although her choosing to stay in their compound gave him an advantage and, if Enda smiled on her, more chance of him gaining a choose-child.

But Viv was not Valen, he reminded himself, and there was no reason for her to act like Valen women, but nor did she act like the elddra. Anfarena had been adamant elddra shunned Valen lovers and yet Viv had taken lovers before, if only for shelter, *and* come close to taking him.

She had reached the front of the queue now and the streets had grown busier while he waited. The other women in the queue returned the appraisal of the passing men but Viv looked straight ahead or at the ground and he did not think it was the arrogant disdain elddra were known for *or* fear, for she had not been like that on the journey. But as he considered her off the cuff remarks about the women who wanted him, he wondered whether he had misunderstood Anfarena's meaning.

Perhaps an elddra's need was for a single, *long-term* lover, the lein-trysts many Valen avoided to maximise their chances of gaining children, and if it *were* what Viv wanted, it strengthened his chances of her choosing him come Glimwing. Her antagonism for his lein would have subsided by then and as his lein continued his own healing, his disapproval of Sehereden's choice would fade. Viv's love for Fariye would help mend the breach as well.

She emerged from the throng at last, still carrying Fariye, who clutched three sticks of shallit. 'Viv couldn't decide,' said Fariye, her face already sticky. 'So we got two of my favourites and some kaest-shallit for you.' She handed him the stick and Viv set her down.

'That was very generous of you, Viv,' he said. 'Thank you.' Men's eyes followed her back to his side and he gave a light-hearted bow and brought her hand to his lips, flipping it at the last moment, to kiss her wrist. It was a more intimate kiss but more importantly told the watchers Sehereden en-Scinta-ril enjoyed the favours of Esh-accom's most beautiful woman.

The metal-wrights proved to be almost as popular as the confectioners, but unlike the confectioners, their customers were exclusively male. 'This way,' said Sehereden, as they edged through the throng. 'These wrights specialise in tribute-charms; the casque-wrights are further along.'

Viv stared at the wares as they passed. Stars, flowers, wriggly shapes she assumed were rills; trees, and birds, including variations on the owl Sehereden had given her. *Tribute-charms*, Sehereden had called them, and the men's interest suggested they were more than trinkets.

'You should trade a chain for Viv too, Ser,' piped Poss. 'She'll need something for all the charms she'll be gifted.'

'I already have, Fari, *and* I've started her collection,' said Sehereden.

'Show me,' said Poss excitedly, and Viv reluctantly pulled it from her pocket. 'You have to *wear* it,' said Poss, grabbing it from her hand and arranging it around Viv's neck so it hung over her jacket. 'It shows *all* the choices you'll have during the festivities. You're going to have *so* many charms, lein, 'cause you're so beautiful but,' she added conspiratorially, 'you should choose Ser. He's the best, apart from da.' She paused. 'Of course, you could choose da.'

Viv picked some imaginary lint from her jacket and it was Sehereden who broke the silence. 'If we're to find a casque, we'd best get on,' he said. 'Vorash isn't going to be kind to us today.'

Viv still saw no clouds, but the air had certainly lost its warmth. Sehereden led them past several more stalls to a less crowded one and as they drew closer, Viv saw why. Its wares were exquisite and, she guessed, expensive.

'I don't need a fancy one,' she muttered, as the metal-wright approached.

'You do,' he replied equably. Poss was silent as her round eyes took in the finely wrought cylinders strung around the stall's shopfront. Some had strands of gold and silver twisted into intricate patterns that reminded Viv of the tether-locks the arsehole had used. Others had gems that flashed as the casques swung in the breeze.

'Do you prefer open or closed work?' asked Sehereden, as the metal-wright hovered.

'Closed.'

'Closed work with dark blue gems to reflect my beautiful companion's eyes,' he said to the metal-wright.

Poss's attention had shifted to the musician across the street and Viv was relieved to see it was not Tarchen or Darch. 'Can I go and listen, Ser?' she asked, tugging at Sehereden's sleeve.

'Yes, but don't wander off,' he said, and handed her some traders.

Viv watched Poss join the circle of spectators. The music was surprisingly sweet, like the Irish tunes her mother had loved. 'He's probably from around the Aranaril,' said Sehereden, following her gaze. 'A long trip, but worth it once the festivities start. Now, I think white gems as well?'

They looked like diamonds and Viv shook her head. 'Just something plain, and I can help pay for it too. Will he take the bracelet as trade?' She reached into her pocket but Sehereden's hand closed over hers.

'Leave it,' he ordered, and turned back to the metalwright with a smile. 'And a chain to keep it safe.'

Viv's lips compressed as Sehereden completed the trade. She had not asked for a casque, especially such an expensive one, she thought angrily. It were as if Sehereden *bought* his way out of the shit he and *his* lein had inflicted on her. It was rude not to at least thank him, but she said nothing as they joined the musician's audience, then Poss donated her traders and they turned for home.

The wind filled with asht-voices and Sehereden scooped up Fariye to quicken their pace. They hurried through the streets along with others keen to take shelter and reached the compound as the rain started. Viv shivered as she followed Sehereden through to the kitchen's warmth. Mereya was baking, the table covered in flour and a massive apron protecting her clothes.

'Best wash your face, Fari, it's covered in shallit,' said Sehereden as he set Poss down by the fire. 'Then maybe Mereya will let you help her.'

'Will you, Mereya?' asked Poss eagerly.

'Come back with a clean face *and* clean hands, and we'll see,' said Mereya.

Poss darted off, and Sehereden picked up a jug and two mugs. 'Is the fire lit in the carving room?' he asked.

Mereya nodded. 'The Syld was working there this morning.'

'Come, Viv,' he said. 'We need to talk.'

Chapter 8

Viv reluctantly followed Sehereden back down the passageway. *We need to talk* was code for interrogation and she regretted not wearing her shirt halter neck style. She had grown careless since she had let trust creep in, she concluded grimly. They passed the bedrooms and washrooms and turned right along one of the wings. Viv had not explored this part of the building, and it revealed more doors and shuttered windows. Most were closed against the rain, but one shutter was ajar, and she glimpsed an internal courtyard, with a roped-off sand-rink in the far corner.

Sehereden stopped at a door and she braced herself, half expecting the arsehole to be waiting inside, ready to extract information about the Waradi as he had long threatened, but the room was empty. It was also gloriously warm, thanks to the fire, and smelled deliciously of wood. Curls of it littered the floor and bigger chunks were stacked against the wall. Viv glanced about. Wood-working tools hung from metal hooks, and a half-finished trinket box sat on a workbench, next to a stack of newly carved chair-backs.

A broad plank of wood ran along one wall, set on wood-blocks, and softened by cushions in emerald and maroon fabric, and Sehereden settled on it and hooked a rudimentary stool closer with his foot to serve as a table. 'I've always liked this room,' he said, as he filled their mugs. 'Sit, Viv, and have some urrut-sa. Mereya's mix of ethris and suril makes hers the best urrut-sa in Esh-accom.'

Viv took the mug he offered and perched on the edge of the bench. The door was closed but unlocked and she visualised the route to the external door, and how the gate latched.

'Maybe I should have said I'd *like* to talk,' he said with a smile. '*Need to talk*, suggests something unpleasant which is the opposite of my intentions.'

Either Sehereden shared Thris's talent for mind-reading or she had completely lost the ability to hide her feelings. She took a sip of the urrut-sa. It tasted of nutmeg, cinnamon, and something like ginger, and while it was not unpleasant, it was not going to be the next *taste sensation*.

'Vorash turns sunny days into icy ones with surprising speed,' said Sehereden conversationally. 'Even the Valen get caught out sometimes. Have you warmed up yet?' He set his mug down and took her hand. His hands were warm and the knot in her stomach eased as his thumb drew soft circles in her palm.

'Vorash doesn't last long before the zadics' settled weather returns,' he continued, as his caress moved to her wrist. 'Some say Vorash is the price Enda extracts for the beauty of the stars, but others say Soaich sends Vorash to remind Enda that *two* gods rule the skies.'

Enda and Soaich; the good always seemed to be paired with its opposite, mused Viv, like Sehereden *and* the arsehole, but it was hard to maintain her angst. The wood-smell was pleasant, the fire-warmth was pleasant, and Sehereden's touch was *more* than pleasant. Viv had not felt as relaxed in living memory and she wondered whether the urrut-sa contained more than spices.

'Wait here for me, Viv?' he said softly. 'There's something I must do. I won't be long.'

Viv nodded, in no hurry to quit the warmth, and idly surveyed the ceiling. The beams had been worked too, but the dimness reduced the carvings to rough outlines, and she went to the window and opened the shutters a crack. It was still icy outside, but the light had strengthened, and Viv's breath caught as she stared upwards.

There was no doubt as to the carver's identity but why carve angels if you loathe everything Angellus? When even the way you say *elddra* is steeped in hatred? Even more shocking was the curve of the angels' wings. It *had* to have been carved by someone who had seen angels in flight.

She wandered to the workbench and stared distractedly at the half-finished trinket box. It was impossible to tell what the whole the design was, but the single wing was complete and so like Thris's she had to grip the bench.

The door opened and she whirled but it was Sehereden with a platter of steaming, delicious-smelling biscuits. 'Come and sample Mereya's *tocki*, Viv. Fari's busy making bird-shaped tocki *because her lein loves birds* and warns you to leave room for them.' The biscuit tasted of retsen, the spices in the urrut-sa, and honey, and was delicious. 'You admire my lein's work, I see,' said Sehereden, as they ate.

'Yes,' said Viv grudgingly.

'You would have liked our sett then, and will in the future, when it's rebuilt.' He nodded at the chair-backs. 'Ataghan already works to replace what's been lost.'

'He's obviously seen the Angellus,' said Viv, her gaze on the beams.

'Paintings, perhaps. The Angellus departed many zadicans ago.'

Which was what Ithreya had said. 'Then he must have been to Astraal,' said Viv. Given the widespread dislike of elddra, she doubted the vals were packed with angel pictures for the arsehole to copy.

'Not that we've discussed.'

Viv looked at him in surprise. 'I thought leins knew everything about each other.'

'We were fifteen when we swore the leinship. How leins lived before they found each other, might or might not be gifted. You've told Fariye very little of your life before you found her.'

Viv swallowed the tocki in painful lump. She should have known Sehereden and the arsehole would have extracted every bit of information she had told Poss or let slip.

Sehereden smiled. 'I didn't bring you here to discuss my lein, or yours, lovely though she is. I wanted time to enjoy your company, and to take the first step to mend the wrongs I've inflicted on you.'

'Your *lein* inflicted.'

'Leins are one, as we've discussed,' said Sehereden smoothly, and took the amè casque from his pocket. It was even lovelier than Viv remembered, its dark blue and frosty gems glowing in the room's muted light. 'It gives me pleasure that you like it,' said Sehereden softly.

'I've never owned anything so beautiful,' she said, and cleared her throat. 'In fact, I've never owned anything beautiful at all. You should have let me help pay for it.'

'You don't pay for gifts, in trade or in kind, and it would have been unwise to advertise your ownership of a Waradi tryst-bracelet. But if you do want to exchange it for traders, let me do it for you.'

Sehereden produced a chain, also of beautiful workmanship, and threaded the casque on. 'For all their beauty, casques are of little worth on their own,' he said, taking her hand. 'I can't replace your amè, Viv, but I can gift you an amè to keep you safe until *you* can replace it.

And my love, along with your lein's, makes for powerful, if temporary, protection.'

He depressed the casque's catch with his thumbnail, half turned the cylinder, slid the catch up, and turned the cylinder back, and then with a click, the curved lid sprang open. Viv's heart missed. She was certain it was the same mechanism as the tether-rope and hatred for the arsehole flared.

'Is it not enough?' asked Sehereden gravely, and Viv dragged her attention back to the casque's contents. It held locks of hair which she guessed were Sehereden and Poss's, and while she knew she had Poss's love, Sehereden seemed to be declaring his as well, or maybe this was just all about sex.

She scrambled up and went to the window and her knuckles whitened on the ledge as he came to her side. 'If there's somewhere you must go to replace your amè, Viv, tell me and I'll take you there.' She shook her head, not trusting herself to speak. None of this was Sehereden's fault! It was just the final crap-heap in a long line of crap-heaps that stretched back to when Kald had first clapped eyes on the red hair and blue eyes of the young Lettie O'Brien.

'*Is* your amè replaceable, Viv?' he asked directly.

'I don't know,' she said thickly. The terrible reality was she might never see Thris again. Her arsehole of a father might have forbidden him from leaving Ezam, or he might be marooned in an alien fold, or he might be dead. The possibilities of the Rynth were bloody uncountable.

'The love of a lein is powerful, but if *my* love isn't enough, we can replace my hair with something else.'

'No!'

'No? My love *is* enough, or it isn't enough, but you don't want to replace it?'

'You don't know me, Sehereden,' she said wildly. 'You can't love someone you don't know!'

'I know enough of you.' Viv shook her head and heard the clicks as the casque closed. Then he slipped the chain over her head, the metal cold against her skin, unlike his fingers as he turned her face to his. 'I know it's hard to carry Astraali blood in the Vales and that those who do sometimes attract more loathing than love, but that doesn't mean they're not worthy of love, that *you're* not worthy of love.'

He kissed her lightly on the lips and held his finger under her chin so she must look at him. 'You already have my love, but I know that to have yours, I must first have your trust. I told you on the journey here that I'm prepared to wait and that holds true. But Fire Zadic begins soon, which I hope you will enjoy, and Lirium follows, then Glimwing with all its promise. And then perhaps, if Enda smiles on us, I *will* trade the Waradi tryst-bracelet, not for coin, but for one you'll wear openly with pride.'

Chapter 9

Ash did not know how long he remained slumped on his knees in the Green Helixai's heart but it was long enough to concoct explanations for the presence of angel bones *and to* dismiss his explanations. All he could think of was that scarabs ate leaf-fall, mantises ate scarabs, sumi ate the animal caste that fell to the forest floor, and glimmers ate *them*. The only bones possible in Ezam were glimmer bones, and *not* mixed with sumi bones in a perfectly shaped cone crowned with angel bones. And most horrifying of all were the blue and white feathers that told him the bones belonged to Senquar-archae.

Angels manifested as flesh, blood, and bone in Ezam, but transformed into turquoise light when they transcended to Crystal Fold and unlike human caste, they left nothing behind. Thris said that human caste remains decayed to breed disease and had to be destroyed, a process so painful to human caste they devised elaborate ceremonies to ease their grief.

Bones and their ceremonies belonged to human caste folds, he told himself, not angel caste ones and yet here, deep in the Green Helixai, was a pile of sumi, glimmer, and angel bones, clearly arranged ceremoniously *and* wreathed in glimmers.

Ash stared down at the glimmers from his perch atop the mound. In the world above they were shy castes rarely seen but here they undulated in a sequence that created a moving ring of colour that, even as he watched, subtly changed. The movement merged the reds, oranges, yellows and greens into the blues and purples, and the blues and purples, into the indigo.

Ash's mouth dried at the revelation. The Blue Helixai tested the unwary with tunnels, the Red with fire, the White with snares of light, and he sensed the Green was about to test him with something just as perilous.

The shimmering ring of indigo glimmers continued their undulations around the bone pile but his attention jerked to the walls. They had begun to ooze, not with the putrid sludge from above, but with something red that he realised in horror was blood. Globules of it beaded the green stone to coalesce into rivulets that painted the walls a fleshy, red-streaked pink.

The blood pooled on the floor and crept across the stone until it lapped the bottom of the bone pile, staining the bones and deepening the glimmers' hue. Then the cavern started to pulse, drawing in and billowing out as if it breathed, but its breaths were uneven and the walls drew ever closer.

Ash whirled, reminded of the Red Helixai and desperate for a way out, but there was none. Then the pile began to shift. Bones rattled down to disappear beneath the surface of the blood and, as the blood-tide rose and engulfed the glimmers, they disappeared too, their ripples telling Ash their undulations continued in the bloody world below.

Ash clamped his wings close to his body in revulsion and then, as if in slow-motion, the bone pile collapsed. The base caved in first and then the upper layers fell, descending in a single, smooth, horizontal motion, as if a sinkhole had opened beneath. Ash gasped in terror as blood filled his eyes, and ears, and mouth, but there was no sensation of drowning despite his downward plunge. Fleshy walls crushed his wings to his back and his arms to his chest, but blood lubricated his passing too until, with shocking suddenness, he landed with a bruising thud on something hard.

His body burned as he sucked in air and light assailed his eyes with a blinding brightness, and then the violent assaults on his senses softened and he could see and breathe normally again. He was on a broad ledge of stone on the side of the Green Helixai, his body untouched by sludge or blood, the surrounding green stone as smooth as glass.

For a while he simply sat and then reluctantly brought his wings forward. They were completely white and he held his breath, expecting to be rent with starbursts and his consciousness to coalesce with the Principae's glory, but nothing happened, and his breath escaped in a long, slow sigh.

He had been the only blue angel in Ezam, then the only Dane with white in his wings, and now it seemed, he was to be the only snowy-winged angel who had failed to transcend. At least his bones had not joined Senquararchae's, he thought morosely, and then faltered as he wondered whether the bone pile had only existed in his mind. He glanced uneasily at the green stone. The Green Helixai had appeared like this early in his time in Ezam but if other angels visited, he wondered how it would appear to them.

He also wondered what the Green Helixai had intended to teach him, for given his experiences in the Blue, Red and White, he knew that his time here had a purpose. The Green Helixai's rank growth, sludge, bones, and blood had certainly reminded him he was more than ether as were Thris and Ky, and he stilled as he pondered whether, having blinked into being together, they must also transcend together, or not at all.

Thris was far from him but Ky was at the Bokos and Ash took to the air, scanning the skies as he flew. Thris had told him of a bird caste in Moonsun Fold that tore its prey apart in mid-air, and Ash felt like that now, as if transcendence hovered just out of sight, waiting to tear *him* apart.

Angels longed for transcendence but it was really a type of death. No angel could be both Dane and Quin-archae, Quin-archae and Tri-archae, Tri-archae and Du-archae, Du-archae and Prime-archae, Prime-archae and Archae, Archae and Principae, Principae and the bright star-stuff of the Great Beyond. Angels had to die in one state to become the other.

He had believed Ezam held no death, but death was all around him, as were new becomings. Even the Great Beyond was not an ending, for Dane sprang from there, or so the Host believed.

He had known none of these things *consciously* before the Green Helixai's dank decay and life-giving blood, and while his new understanding failed to explain why he was white-winged, he now understood Prime-archaes Serith and Mirek's fascination with Senquar-archae. Hope woke that the Prime-archaes' understanding might aid him, and he quickened his wingbeats, leaving a trail of translucence behind him that was no longer blue, but a glittering white.

Only Ky studied at the table under the window, and he remained silent long after Ash had finished speaking. Ash did not mind; simply being with Ky was a comfort, as was the gloomy shelves of scrolls and the distant footsteps of other angelic scholars. They were familiar things in a familiar place, where the stone did not suddenly shift under his feet, and where Ky's love and Prime-archae Mirek's kindness remained unchanging.

Ky looked subtly different to Ash, and he sensed Ky's competitive need to best his fellow Dane had transformed into a need to help them. It was a change that marked entry into the Archae and one thought necessary to transcendence, and yet Ky remained Dane as well. 'You have visited all the Helixai now,' said Ky at last, 'and they have gifted you the white plumage of transcendence.'

'But *not* transcendence,' said Ash.

'Logically, it means there must be more to do,' said Ky.

'Logically, it means I am unworthy of transcendence.'

'*Logically*, there could be lots of reasons you have not transcended,' persisted Ky.

'Including unworthiness.'

'Do you know how many steps I have taken in the Bokos this cycle?' asked Ky abruptly. Ash shrugged, and Ky grinned. 'Neither do I. Oh, I know how many from particular shelves to here, and sometimes it can be several thousand, but I have given up keeping over all totals. The Bokos is enormous, Ash,' he said and gestured expansively.

'And filled with scrolls that are not always true?' asked Ash.

Ky nodded. 'The scrolls contain angel lore written by angels over the eons of Ezam's existence. Some wrote their wisdom clearly, some as if they rambled through the glis, and some, no doubt, wrote nothing and kept their wisdom to themselves. We know of Senquar-archae only because he was written of, but there might be other blue angels that no one wrote of, whose time in Ezam mirrored yours.'

Ash hoped Ky was right but his dread remained. 'I do not know if I should stay,' he said. 'I do not know the risks I pose. I fear Senquar-archae's bones might be a warning.'

'Of what?'

'Of a destruction I might wreak.' He tried to smile and failed. 'The sense of death was strong in the Helixai, Ky, but so was the sense of rebirth, and one precedes the other.'

Ky's arms came around him and held him close, and Ash's tension eased as he inhaled Ky's sweetness. They stood enfolded for a long time, and it was how Prime-archae Mirek found them. The Prime-archae's face revealed his shock at Ash's plumage but his smile held its usual welcome. 'I see there is much to discuss,' he said. 'Let us begin.'

Chapter 10

Viv lay in bed through the long night and listened to the rain's rush and gurgle down the stone gutters. Neither Sehereden nor the arsehole appeared at breakfast and Poss's face showed her disappointment at not being able to show Viv more of the traders' stalls. Viv was disappointed too, but over the delayed search for her mother.

'I can teach you some dances,' said Poss, 'but it would be better if Ser played his yu.' Tormis came in with a load of wood, dumped it near the hearth, and shook the water from his cape. 'Do you know when da and Ser are coming back?' asked Poss.

'I'm not expectin' them this day, Fari. The Syld says the horses need a gallop, and him and his lein have gone up the Esha. I think he's taken some of his band too.'

'He never told me he was going,' said Poss, in a small voice.

'You know your da, Fari. Likes the feel of the rain on his face.'

'We don't need music to practise dancing, Poss,' said Viv, glad the arsehole was far away. 'We can hum or sing. It will be fun,' she added.

As it turned out, they did neither. Ithreya returned and she knew how to play the yu and the pipe, and even Poss could play simple tunes on both. To add to Viv's sense of inadequacy, the dances turned out to be long and intricate. She had to half crouch to dance with Poss, and Ithreya soon took Poss's place, leaving Poss to make the music.

Viv had never danced much, let alone with a woman, and Ithreya was taller than Viv, and a whole lot curvier. There were dances that required they embrace like lovers and Viv kept her gaze on Ithreya's many tribute-charms. Stars, birds, and flowers, all of them exquisite workmanship. She counted over a dozen but there were probably more hidden under Ithreya's shirt.

Ithreya described each of the dances as they practised. The Argine-ley with its fast beat, mirrored the Cades' thunder to the Vales' floor; the rill-ley, with its the slow weave of cross-over steps, reflected the rills' meander to join the Eshacade; and the Fire-ley, with its solitary steps and intimate embraces echoed the courtships and passion of the festivities.

Viv was glad to break for their midday meal, her head full of dance steps she would probably forget before she had a chance to use them. The arsehole had the right idea about getting some fresh air, she decided, and resolved to start the search for her mother after the meal. The rain had dwindled to drizzle anyway.

Tormis joined them at the table, his bony hands wrapped around a mug of semna, which Viv deduced was heated urrut-sa. He was keen for news from Ithreya because, in some convoluted web of relationships, Tormis's sister was a si-tryst in a sett that another si-tryst had visited, before the second si-tryst had gone to Ithreya's choose-brother's sett, and Ithreya's choose-brother was now with his and Ithreya's kin in Esh-accom.

Viv had conjured a male version of Ithreya, with blonde hair and china-blue eyes, before she recalled choose-children siblings might not be biologically related at all. Ithreya had referred to her late father as a *seed-father*, so her mother must have at least named him as the father, but given Ithreya had a *choose*-brother, her father had not lein-trysted. Her brother's mother had simply *chosen* Ithreya's father to leave her son with.

The fold's child-rearing practices were as complicated as their dance steps, but the men's want for children filled her with envy. It was not about proving manhood by knocking-up as many women as possible, but about being judged *worthy* to be named as father. Hence the tournaments, she suddenly realised, which demonstrated the men's virility in a very public way.

But Fire Zadic was about more than puffed chests and flexed muscles; there were tribute-charms, and dancing, and the winning of favours. But why was Fire Zadic so important when children could be seeded anytime? And Lirium and Glimwing were important too, from what Sehereden had said.

It was a pity folds did not provide Tourist Information pamphlets at their rift exits, she concluded dryly. *Places of Interest, Local Customs, Things to Avoid*, like turning up looking like one of the fold's least desirable citizens.

She grimaced and pushed her chair from the table. 'I'm going for a walk,' she said.

'Not much to see,' said Mereya, appearing with the customary bowl of fruit. 'The wrights are shuttered. Best wait for the day after next. Vorash should ease by then.'

Viv forced a smile. 'I need to stretch my legs.'

'I'll get a cape from the store, then,' said Tormis. 'It'll keep the worse of it off.'

'Get two, will you?' said Ithreya. 'I promised to show Viv around. Or, maybe we need three,' she added, smiling at Poss.

'I'm baking again today, Fari,' said Mereya. 'Like to make some more tocki? Or would you rather go out and get cold and wet?'

Poss's grin made her choice clear and Viv was relieved, but she would have preferred Ithreya stayed at the compound too. It would be quicker to reconnoitre alone and do a more thorough search later, not take the stroll Ithreya probably envisaged.

Ithreya turned out to be both a quick walker and a mine of information, and Viv was soon glad of her company. The drizzle continued, and it remained chill, but the capes were hooded and voluminous, and Viv was snug inside. Hers reached almost to the ground, for it was big on her, and with her hood up, she looked no different to anybody else on the street, not that there were many.

Viv discovered that Esh-accom's visitors were accommodated in a variety of ways. If they traded goods such as leather-work, trinkets, and toys, they procured stalls as close as possible to Esh-accom's wrights and slept there. Those of lesser wealth clustered in Soaich Square, a strip of open ground sunwise of Axian. These were often wagoners who, for a price, exhibited strange or exotic beasts, or traded lesser quality woven stuffs such as rugs and cushions. They set maarks and slept close to their wagons.

Those with more trade who came to compete in the tournaments or to enjoy the festivities, might stay with their kin, or if they had no kin in Esh-accom, trade for spare rooms in a compound. Many had unused rooms their owners were happy to earn coin for, although not the arsehole apparently.

77

'Sehereden says his lein keeps his compound's rooms empty as a reminder of the Ascadi and Waradi's brutality,' said Ithreya. Viv grimly contemplated she had no need of reminders; images of Esh-embrin's charred bodies and Poss huddled in the crap-filled cave seared into her brain forever. She had no idea what the Valen fought over but whatever it was, the fight had no rules, given the massacre at Esh-embrin and the one led by the arsehole.

They emerged into an open area of rain-washed cobblestones that looked like the European city squares Viv had seen on TV. 'This is Axian, Esh-accom's centre,' said Ithreya. 'It's full of stalls come Fire Zadic, and the tournaments are held here too.' Ithreya stopped and gestured as she slowly turned. 'The Syld's compound is behind us in Miraj Quarter, Merint Quarter is half-cloudwise from here, Anaten Quarter half-sunwise, and Shelin Quarter, also called the Old Quarter, half-starwise.'

'So, clockwise it's Miraj, Merint, Anaten, and Shelin *or* the Old Quarter,' murmured Viv as she tried to sort them.

'*Clockwise*?'

'This way,' said Viv, waving her arm in a circular motion as if the description were perfectly normal in a fold with no clocks.

'I've not heard that term before,' said Ithreya. Viv frowned, as if she struggled to remember Esh-accom's quarters rather than cursed her own stupidity. She would be asking how many *hours* it took to walk all the way around Esh-accom next. But the real problem was not her verbal slip-ups but the lack of hotels. It meant there was no obvious place to check whether a red-haired, blue-eyed woman, had just booked in.

The drizzle continued, smudging the surrounding buildings, and making them look even more like a film set. A caped-figure hurried along on the opposite side of the square and disappeared down a pathway between the buildings, but apart from him or *her*, they had Axian to themselves.

'Do they keep a list of who enters Esh-accom?' asked Viv as they set off across the square.

'The Wall Guard record the traders because traders pay rents to secure trading rights, and they record the tournament's competitors, so Esh-accom's Sylds can draw up the schedules. The Sylds try to make the bouts as exciting as possible to maximise the wager-tributes.'

It sounded like a nice, cosy, little money-making scheme, thought Viv, and useless in her quest to find her mother. 'If your mother looks like you, she'd be noticed,' continued Ithreya, guessing Viv's thoughts.

'That's what Drasen said.'

'In which case, it might be useful to visit my kin's compound. Mecenth's lived here all his life and knows most of what goes on, including comings and goings. He's friends with the Wall Guards too.'

Viv nodded, feeling more encouraged. A wagon lumbered from the street to their left and they stopped to let it pass. It veered towards the Merint Quarter and Viv guessed it headed to Soaich Square. It had a birdman-like creature painted on the back and Viv was reminded of the wagon she had seen on her first night.

Ithreya led the way into a narrow street of close-packed buildings made gloomy by the dull light. Sodden strips of material flapped against shuttered windows, and birds perched under eaves, feathers fluffed against the cold.

'Are traders allowed to bring Lefer into Esh-accom?' asked Viv as they walked.

'Yes, and no.' Ithreya smiled briefly. 'Esh-accom's Sylds want as many traders here as possible to add to Esh-accom's coffers and, of course, traders want to be here too, to add to *their* coffers. Those without craft-skills craft bring *entertainments*.

'In exchange for your traders, you can see *exotic creatures captured from the far vals by brave adventurers*, or the *highly elusive parien that few Valen have ever witnessed*, or other *strange and wondrous mixes engendered by the Angellus*.' She half shook her head. 'I have no interest in such things, Viv, but I know from those who have, that the creatures are mostly Lefer, artfully or not so artfully disguised.'

'But it's cruel,' exclaimed Viv. 'Lefer shouldn't be locked up, or made to fight, or mistreated, just to make *mon*—to make coin.'

'That's what the Syld thinks too, according to his lein,' said Ithreya mildly.

'But what happens to the Lefer after the festivities?' pursued Viv. 'Are they released?'

'They might be. It would be pretty troublesome to keep them until next Fire Zadic but I've also heard they're used for meat.' Viv jerked to a stop and Ithreya's wet hand gripped her arm. 'You can't do anything about it, Viv. Once the wagoners have paid their rent, they have the right to make coin like everyone else.'

'And what bloody rights do the Lefer have?'

'You can't do anything about it,' repeated Ithreya. Viv remained immovable and Ithreya softened her voice. 'Sehereden told me you freed Lefer from a gaming-cage, but that was high in the vals. It's different here. Even if the

80

Syld or his lein wanted to free the Lefer, they couldn't. Esh-accom's Sylds have always allowed the *entertainments* and that's not going to change.'

Chapter 11

The compound that belonged to Ithreya's kin turned out to be a smaller, humbler version of the arsehole's with stables along one side of the front, a pretty bush in its centre, and a courtyard at the back framed by the building's wings. There was no carved wood in the passageways, and the furniture in the hall was unadorned but Viv still thought it had a homelier feel.

It might have been due to the people who gathered in the hall's warmth, not just fighting men hoping for Fire Zadic's *gifts,* but older Valen, teenagers, and small children. Drasen was there too and Ithreya's choose-brother Galian, and neither hid their delight at Ithreya and Viv's arrival.

A grey-haired woman fussed about helping them out of their capes, and then a queue formed to greet them. Ithreya had only been gone a day but they hugged her as if she had been absent for years. Viv escaped the hugs but the smiles she received were surprisingly warm.

Mecenth was not there but expected back soon and Drasen collected a jug of semna, and Ithreya and Galian cups and a platter of tocki, and they headed off to a room in one of the wings. It had low tables, chairs and couches, and another fire. The only thing it lacked was a TV but there were instruments like guitars propped against the wall.

Women stitched near the fire and a man carved wood beside them, cloth spread at his feet to catch the chips. A group of boys occupied another section of the floor, sitting cross-legged around a game that looked like checkers. The arsehole's compound was nothing like this, Viv concluded disparagingly, although it might have been before his sett had been murdered and she suddenly wondered whether grief fed his hatred of her as much as her Waradi taint, then shrugged. She was starting to sound like a prison shrink.

'Viv?' It was Drasen and she realised she still stood while they had all found seats. He patted a spot on the couch beside him and she sat awkwardly. Ithreya made a quick round of the room with the tocki and Galian poured the drinks. The rain had returned with a vengeance and for a moment, only its slosh in the courtyard gutters filled the silence.

'My choose-sister could have picked a kinder day to show you Esh-accom's sights,' said Galian pleasantly.

'It was my idea,' said Viv. 'I hate being stuck inside.' Galian's blond hair and blue eyes made him so like Ithreya, Viv found it hard to make eye contact. They could have been twins.

'Since our discussion on our journey here, I've asked those in Esh-accom about your mother,' said Drasen. 'There seems to be four or six red-haired women in Esh-accom, depending on who you speak to, but they all seem to be elddra. Is your mother elddra too?'

Viv shook her head. 'Elddra can't …' She stopped. She had almost said elddra cannot have children because she certainly could not, but if the Angellus had produced the Astraali, and the Astraali the Du-Daimon, it meant at least some male and female daimon were fertile.

'Elddra can't what?' pursued Drasen.

Galian and Ithreya were intent on her answer too but Ithreya would pass on whatever she said to Sehereden, and Sehereden to the arsehole. 'Nothing,' said Viv, with a shrug. 'Did they say where these elddra lived?'

'Two in Merint, two in this quarter, and two in the Old Quarter,' said Drasen. 'The two in the Old Quarter are recent arrivals and thought to have been forced into Esh-accom by the fighting.'

'I think Sehereden's already spoken with them,' said Ithreya thoughtfully. 'But he asked them about you, Viv, not about your mother. It was while you were healing at Tahsin's sett, after the Waradi hurt you. But the elddra knew nothing of you, which Sehereden thought was odd, because elddra are all supposed to know each other.'

Drasen and Galian's shock told Viv they knew nothing about her being in Waradi hands, and Ithreya obviously knew nothing about Viv's prior dealings with the arsehole. The rain no longer pounded down, which was fortunate, because it meant she could make her escape. 'I'm going to continue my walk,' she said, and got to her feet. 'You don't need to come, Ithreya, given the rain. Maybe you could ask Mecenth what he knows on my behalf. I'll be leaving soon and need to familiarise myself with Esh-accom so I can make a proper search when the weather improves.'

Ithreya looked unconvinced and Viv's tight throat meant her angel part was not convinced either, probably because she had left out the bit about visiting Soaich Square. 'I don't think you should go alone,' said Ithreya.

'I've survived worse places,' said Viv with a forced smile.

'I'm concerned about you getting lost,' said Ithreya. 'Esh-accom's streets are as tangled as a leaf-lilter's nest. Drasen or Galian should go with you, or I will.' There was no mistaking Ithreya's determination, despite her gentle tone, and Viv chose Galian as her guide. Her choice sent a message to both men but Galian had the advantage because he knew far less about her.

Galian's company turned out to be as pleasant as his sister's, but wind had added itself to the miserable weather, making it hard to speak. Viv told him she wanted to see the Merint Quarter and then they pulled their hoods low, and walked in silence. The conditions were even worse once they left the buildings' shelter. They fought their way across Axian's exposed paving to another street and its shelter soon gave way to what Viv assumed was Soaich Square.

It might have been a pleasant grassy area before the rain and wagons, but it was now a barren sprawl of mud, cut with water-filled wheel ruts. The beasts that pulled the wagons huddled together in pens, backs to the squalls, and smoke from fires set under make-shift canopies, tainted the air with the smell of burnt fat.

Viv stepped from the path but Galian caught her arm. 'That's not the best way to go,' he said. 'Your mother won't be here.'

'I need to check,' said Viv and gently disengaged herself. The wagons had been set side on, probably to advertise their wares, and Viv picked her way along their length. They were covered with garishly painted canvass awnings that depicted bird-like creatures, some more human-looking than others. One had daubs of orange paint that mimicked fire and the creature hung above it, black wings outstretched.

'We're not openin' yet, Valen,' came a voice. Viv started, having not noticed the tarpaulin slung at the wagon's end where men warmed themselves around a fire. 'Come back at the festivities and you'll see a sight that'll be amazin' and delightin' those fortunate enough to be witness.'

Viv retraced her steps glad her hood hid her face. She sensed the men's hard eyes follow her but it was the Lefer's plight that made her shiver. 'You're cold,' said Galian. 'Perhaps it's best we return to my compound.' Viv said nothing even when his wet hand clasped hers. In a world of abusive ment, the Lefer were as powerless as she had been and she refused to abandon them as she had been abandoned.

Viv slid her hand free as soon as they reached Axian. 'Thank you for guiding me in such terrible weather,' she managed to say. 'I've decided to return to Sehereden en-Scinta-ril's compound.'

'I'll escort you,' said Galian.

'No!' She forced a smile. 'I already feel guilty for dragging you out in this rain. Thank you again,' she said and before he could object, set off quickly across the cobbles, not pausing until she was in Miraj. Then she slid behind a stall and peered back. Galian still stared after her, as if he debated whether to follow, and she waited until he turned back towards Anaten, then hastened back to Axian and headed into the Old Quarter.

Her mother was hardly likely to be wandering about in the rain but even the awful weather was preferable to the arsehole's compound. She contemplated his obnoxious behaviour as she strode along and was taken by surprise when the street suddenly exited into another square. It had trees, seats and fountain that made it very different to Axian's open cobblestones.

The trees were so tall it seemed odd someone had planted them in the middle of a town but their sheltering branches reduced the rain to musical plinks that reminded Viv of Thris's obsession with resonance. Her yearning for him was so intense she stumbled to a stop and then her skin pricked.

Life on the streets had honed Viv's awareness of being watched and she wrenched her hood back to better scan. The murky weather did not help and she heard the footsteps first. The figures that appeared from the street behind her had been too far away to be the watchers and they stopped when they saw her. The hoods of their capes hid their faces and there was a hiatus before one pulled their hood back.

Viv's heart leapt. Red hair! But the woman's hair was wavy, not curly, and streaked with grey. Her mother might be grey by now too, reasoned Viv, but the woman's face was all wrong. The one who had revealed herself touched her companion's arm and the second woman pulled her hood back.

The elddra Sehereden had spoken to, guessed Viv, but she did not feel like hanging around for a chat and they approached cautiously, as if they expected her to make a dash for it too. The elddra who had revealed herself first was calm, but her companion's hands twisted convulsively, and Viv's tension ratcheted up.

'I am Anfarena,' the calm one said, 'and this is Anetherey.' She touched her companion again as she introduced her, but it was a firmer touch now, and Anetherey's hands quietened.

'I'm Viv.'

'Violet Iris Vacia,' said Anfarena clearly. 'Beautiful names it is a shame not to use. Then again, I understand why, as a stranger here, you might like to keep things as *simple* as possible. Anetherey and I are strangers here too, but we know the *dangers* and how to *avoid* them.'

Anfarena paused, giving Viv time to digest what she had said. She might seem to refer to Esh-accom, but Viv knew the message went deeper than that. 'I'm not intending to stay,' said Viv. 'I'm searching for my mother and if she's not here I'm leaving.'

Anetherey grew agitated again and Anfarena actually gripped her arm this time. Viv knew she was the cause of the upset, but did not know why, and glanced back the way she had come. Maybe the arsehole's compound was a better deal after all. 'Would you honour us by sharing our food?' asked Anfarena formally. 'Our accommodation is close. There are no others there,' she added.

It seemed churlish to refuse but Viv castigated herself as she followed them past the fountain and across the square. The last thing she needed was another batch of questions that required mental gymnastics to answer without lying. She hoped she would get some sort of useful information about her mother in return but that was not all she hoped for. Being an outsider was hard anywhere, but this fold's antagonism for elddra was the icing on a very crappy cake. Meeting elddra meant she was no longer totally alone and they might even help her, *if* they believed she were one of them.

Chapter 12

The elddra's accommodation was the least grand Viv had been in, but it was warm, and the room Anetherey took her to was comfortable. There was a couch, a table and chairs, and a chest against the wall, with wooden cylinders on it. The window shutters were partly ajar, so Viv could see how dark it was getting outside, and Anetherey hung their capes on wall-hooks before she disappeared back up the passageway.

Anfarena directed her to a seat and Viv had the curious sensation of being in a principal's office. The elddra was clearly used to being in charge but given the open window, Viv reminded herself she could leave any time she chose.

'Our sett at the Bracken-ril is more *pleasing* but circumstances dictate we reside here for a time,' said Anfarena.

'The fighting, you mean?'

'Among other things.'

'I'm unclear what the fighting's about,' said Viv, as Anetherey returned with a platter of delicately swirled biscuits and a jug of pinkish liquid. Anfarena filled an engraved cup for her and placed a biscuit on a matching plate but it was Anetherey who served Anfarena.

Hierarchies made Viv uneasy, especially where there was unquestioning obedience. Rim's control of the gang; Kald's control of Thris; the arsehole's control of Sehereden; if the elddra's setup were the same, Viv would not be hanging around.

'Violet Iris Vacia asks why the Valen fight,' said Anfarena, as Anatherey settled at the table.

'The Valen are war-like,' said Anetherey contemptuously. 'This time, it was the crossing of crests and once the bloodshed started, *honour* required it continued.'

'What caused the fighting last time?' asked Viv curiously.

Anetherey shrugged. 'Horses, women.' Viv had a feeling Anfarena did not agree, that the reasons for the violence were more complex and that Anfarena tested her in some way, but Viv concentrated on her drink. Despite its watermelon smell, it tasted like dry white wine.

'You may be aware that Sehereden en-Scinta-ril came here seeking information about you,' said Anfarena.

'So I've heard,' said Viv, now fascinated by her biscuit.

'He told us your name and that you denied being from the Vales or Astraal,' said Anfarena.

'Sehereden thought my name was short for Vivreya. I corrected him.'

'And you told him you were not from the Vales or Astraal?'

'No,' said Viv; she had actually told Poss. 'I told him I was looking for my mother who disappeared when I was ten,' she said, wanting to steer the conversation in a more useful direction. 'Esh-accom has lots of visitors during the tournaments and festivities. I thought it would be a good place to look. I was wondering whether you knew of her. She would be mistaken for an elddra because she looks like me, although she might be grey by now.'

'All elddra in the Vales are known to each other,' said Anfarena crisply. 'We do not mistake those of our blood.'

'Others might.'

'As they might mistake you.'

'I've been mistaken for all sorts of things,' said Viv with a shrug. 'So, you know nothing of my mother? Her name's Violet, but she calls herself Lettie.'

'You share a name?'

'Just a first name. Iris is after my grandmother, and Vacia after my great grandmother.' Viv took another sip of her drink aware she had just dug herself into a hole. She had no idea how elddra were named *or* Valen, but given the Valen's focus on seed- and choose-fathers, mothers probably did not get a look in.

'And did these others of your line also look like you?'

'Yes.'

'And were they elddra?'

'No.'

'And are *you* elddra?'

'I've been called many things in my life,' said Viv and glanced at Anetherey. Her pale amethyst eyes held a hunger Viv found disturbing.

'You haven't answered my question,' said Anfarena.

'It's simplest to let people believe what they want to believe about me.'

'Even if those beliefs are incorrect?'

'I have no control over what people believe *or* how they act on their beliefs,' said Viv, failing to hide her bitterness.

'Sehereden en-Scinta-ril said you had sworn leinship with Ataghan en-Scinta-ril's choose-daughter,' said Anfarena, abruptly changing tack. 'Was that incorrect too?'

'She *is* my lein,' said Viv, with an unexpected surge of pride.

'He also implied you travelled with a companion.'

'Did he?' said Viv, batting a question back.

'Yes, and implied your companion was not elddra.'

Viv's mind raced. Sehereden had obviously told the elddra Viv was not alone but had not revealed more, or had he? Maybe Anfarena spun a web of lies to catch her in, and Viv wondered whether she should leave. It was completely dark outside now and the drizzle had changed back to rain.

'I think you are avoiding telling me the truth,' said Anfarena softly.

'My life would be a hell of a lot easier if that were possible,' snapped Viv and got to her feet. 'I thought you might be able to help find my mother but that seems unlikely.'

'It is more likely than you think.'

'Why? Because you're not telling me the truth either?'

Anfarena half-smiled. 'Like you, I find that particular skill difficult. Please sit again, Violet Iris Vacia, and maybe we can both speak more plainly.'

'It's Viv,' said Viv, sitting reluctantly.

'I know you did not grow up in Astraal,' said Anfarena smoothly, 'so your knowledge of it must come from your mother, or the Valen, or from other *imperfect* sources. Even some of those who call the Sacred City home, are ignorant of its true history. Let me share it with you. You might find it useful.

'The Wheel, as the Valen call it, was once exclusively their home. They lived peaceably here, each people within their own Vale, until my forebears, the Angellus, arrived. The Angellus desired beauty and they found it in the Sacred Lake and the symmetry of the eight cades it feeds. They found it in the Vale's women too, for the Angellus brought with them no females of their own kind.

'The Valen visited the Sacred Lake, not just when Called, but to enjoy its beauty. The Grey Fire was the Grey Mist then, and similar to the mist cloudwise of the Argine, though denser and more chill. The Angellus persuaded the most beautiful Valen women to stay with them, not that they took much persuasion. The Angellus were as beautiful as the beauty they sought. Slow to age, winged, and wise in all but one thing, of which I will speak shortly.

'They built a magnificent city to house themselves and the red-haired, blue-eyed mothers of their children. Their idea of female beauty was very particular, but those traits were not common in The Wheel even then and so, as time went on, they chose blue-eyed, *darker-haired* women instead.

'They called the children they seeded Daimon, for being half-Valen, they lacked the perfection of the Angellus. The dilution of beauty made the Angellus increasingly uneasy and they questioned the *unnaturalness* of what they had created and stopped seeding Daimon. Some even sent their Valen women back to the Vales.

'The Angellus came to believe they had tainted the very thing that had drawn them here and pondered the dangers of creatures whose baser human substance they had enhanced with divine sensibilities. A longing grew in the Angellus to seek another *unsullied* place, where there would be no repeat of their mistakes, and so they left.'

Viv nodded; it was a more detailed, personalised version of what Ithreya had said.

'The Daimon, like their forebears, chose wives from amongst the Valen, and called *their* children the Du-Daimon but, as time went on, some Daimon also became uneasy at what they had created. Others of their kind shrugged off their concerns and changed the name of the city and Sacred Lake to Astraal and named themselves the Astraali.

'They imposed barriers to the Valen's visits and insinuated themselves as the Sacred Lake's true and rightful guardians, and those who shared the Angellus's unease saw their fears played out before their eyes. They withdrew to their Halls to spend their time in search, and what they search for, Violet Iris Vacia, is the way out. The door the Angellus used to depart has been lost, and the Du-Daimon remain trapped here, forced to watch the destruction unfold.'

Anfarena took a sip of her drink. 'I am Du-Daimon, as is Anetherey, as are all elddra in the Vales. We were seeded by those who still call themselves Daimon. The Astraali continue to seed children, and keep their daughters close, for the Angellus's beauty can still be glimpsed in them, but they expel their sons.

'Their sons are violent, as if their human and divine elements war with each other, and it is their sons who feed the wars here. The *unwiseness* of the Angellus scarred The Wheel but they are no longer here to witness it. The Daimon wish they were no longer here to witness it either. They search the sacred peak, the lake and all things the Angellus wrote, for the path the Angellus took, and we, their daughters, search the Vales.'

Viv stared down at the table. The elddra *were* spies but not in the way the Valen thought, and her timing, as usual, was exquisite. She had turned up looking like an elddra when the havoc male angel-mix wreaked made the Valen's fear and suspicion of outsiders extreme. She really had hit the jackpot of *folds-not-to-visit*, she concluded bitterly, when she had escaped the suffocation of the last place and landed here.

94

'I have gifted you things known only to elddra that might aid your search,' continued Anfarena. 'All these things are true but let us now explore things that might not be true.' Anfarena's regard intensified. 'If your mother looks like you, you would have been seeded in Astraal, but as you are no longer there, she must have birthed you in a sett so isolated, even the Scharii failed to visit it. Had they visited it, she would have been *persuaded* back to Astraal and you would have been taken with her.

'But even *if* you were raised in an isolated sett, for you *and* your mother to have escaped the Sharii's attention *and* ours, you must have remained there until recently, and if your mother is no longer there, she can only be in Astraal.' Anfarena paused. 'Of course, these things assume you are elddra and I do not believe you are.'

Viv was not about to blurt out her life's story but her throat tightened at the thought of concocting an alternative one

'I am not going to ask for your trust, Violet Iris Vacia,' continued Anfarena, her gaze unwavering, 'though I hope you will soon grant it, but I will say this: as the children of the Du-Daimon, we revere our Angellus blood by shunning violence but those who take the Astraali name have no such reservations. There are dangers for you in Astraal if you go there unprotected, and there are dangers for you here in the Vales, as I suspect you have discovered. Your best chance of finding your mother, *and* remaining safe, lies with us.'

Chapter 13

Viv mulled over Anfarena's words as she perched, wet and uncomfortable, in the trees at the edge of the square. She had told Anfarena she needed time to think, but three things were already glaringly obvious: Anfarena knew Viv was not elddra, she had no idea where Viv's mother was, and given Viv had not been *persuaded* by the Astraali to stay in their city, she must have come through the magic door the Daimon, Du-Daimon and elddra were desperate to find.

Viv pushed the wet curls from her eyes. She knew how to find and use rifts but it was pot-luck where she ended up. And supposing she *did* lead those who wanted to quit The Wheel through a rift like a modern-day Moses? They might exit into Sand Fold, or the cat creature's fold, or somewhere worse. She did not think her *beloved* father would be impressed with them trooping into Ezam either.

Then there was the whole issue of transference which the Angellus had committed on a grand scale. One way or another they had created conflict by stealing the Valens' most sacred site, causing deadly weather changes like the ice-fire, and leaving behind hybrids despised by everyone. And in the end, the Angellus had been so disgusted with their handiwork they had up and left.

Viv grunted. It was like going on a picnic in the Ranges and leaving all your trash behind. Anfarena was right about the dangers in the Vale but Astraal did not sound like a barrel of laughs either, given Anfarena offered her safety there in return for the keys to the door of a rift out.

By the time Viv had eased her cramped body down the tree, the only sound was the pit of rain against the cobbles. It was very dark and given Vorash, there would be no constellation, which was just as well given what Viv had in mind. But the gloom also made it hard to tell how late it was. The windows shuttered against the weather hid whether people were still around or had taken themselves off to bed. Sehereden and the arsehole probably still galloped about in the Vale, but Ithreya would be worrying and Viv hoped she did not send Tormis in search of her.

She broke into a jog but slowed again when she reached Axian so that any witnesses only saw a caped figure, hurrying to escape the soggy conditions, and when she reached the street Galian had escorted her down, ran again. Her excellent night vision made it easy to pick when the buildings gave way to Soaich Square, and she stopped and scanned. The area was even muddier now and she debated whether to discard her cape and change her shirt to a halter neck.

If push came to shove, the mud would make running hard, but flying was riskier given the Lefer had probably been captured with darts which meant their captors were good at shooting things out the sky. The possibility of being dragged unconscious through the streets, *with her wings exposed*, was too awful to contemplate.

Her hand fastened on her amè casque and she opened and closed it several times. Given it was probably the same lock the arsehole used on her, she hoped it was used on the Lefers' cages too.

She could smell no smoke, which she hoped meant the men slept, but given their shabbiness, they might have run out of wood. She recalled the first two wagons and the last had Lefer-like creatures daubed on their awnings, but there were a lot more wagons now and she stared at them in dismay.

The gloom had swallowed the crude artwork on the first but she crept forward, slid between the sodden awning and the cage, and fumbled for the lock. Nothing. Shit! It must be on the other side *where the men slept*. At least the miserable chitter from the cage confirmed the creature *was* a Lefer. She just hoped it had the wit escape once she found the bloody lock!

She slipped around the wagon's other side and her heart lurched as she bruised her knuckles on a square-shaped block of metal. Then her fingers brushed something the right shape and she found the lever on the side and with shaking hands, pushed it in, half turned the cylinder, pushed the catch up, and turned the cylinder back. The clicks sounded as loud as thunder, but the door came loose and she wrenched it open.

She had no time to see what happened next, just hastened to the second wagon. The sound of wings told her the first Lefer had gone and she felt a wave of relief. One down, two to go. Knowing where to look made the second break-in easier and this Lefer was quicker to quit its cage but its leathery wings buffeted her and worse of all, it cawed as it flapped away.

The cry might have gone unnoticed during the day when Esh-accom's streets were full of traders, but the night was quiet and Viv's instincts screamed to get the hell out of there even as her brain argued the traders would rush to the *empty cages* first.

The glow of a lantern broke the darkness behind her and curses erupted as she desperately tried to work out which wagon had been daubed with the orange paint to mimic fire. She still had time, she told herself, but then a hand slammed down on her shoulder. 'Got ya, ya stinkin' thief!'

Viv ducked and twisted with such speed that the man was left holding an empty cape, then took off between the wagons, but it was even darker there and her arms windmilled as she careered into boxes and barrels and sent them flying. There were more shouts and the wet thump of pursuing feet but she reached the cobbled street and picked up speed.

Her thoughts raced on ahead as she pounded along. She wanted to head back to Axian knowing she would be faster in the open but so would they and they might force her down some dead-end street. She swerved right at the first junction, left at the next, then right using the techniques Thris had taught her to maintain her pace. The sound of pursuit lessened, as if some of the traders had given up, but they might have split up to cut her off.

Viv sensed she was in Anaten but returning to Ithreya and Galian's compound was not an option and nor was heading back to the arsehole's. She could not risk them being confronted by a mob of angry traders *or* knowing about her night time activities.

The trees in the Old Quarter were her best bet, *if* she could get far enough ahead to scale them unseen. She could wait out the night there and fly away if cornered, but Ithreya was right; the streets *were* tangled and the traders would know Esh-accom better than she did. Her breath scalded her throat as she ran on, recognising nothing.

She needed to get back to Axian to orientate herself and she increased her speed, took several more turns, and panting hard, burst into Axian. The street to the Old Quarter was several blocks to her left and she fled across the square and, as shouts sounded behind her, swerved down the street to the Old Quarter without slowing.

The cobbles were slick and her feet went from under her, the shock smashing the air from her lungs as she slewed across the stone, but she scrambled up and dashed on. The fall meant the men had gained on her and she ran for her life but then a shadow launched from an alleyway, smacked a suffocating hand over her mouth, and wrenched her back into the darkness.

The attack was so sudden Viv hardly comprehended what had happened. Her captor dragged her swiftly up an alleyway, shouldered open a compound gate, stopped its slam with his heel, and threw them both deep into the wall's shadows.

'Stay silent,' he hissed, his hand still fastened over her mouth, his arm clamping her hard up against him.

Feet pounded past the end of the alleyway and then returned more slowly and stopped. There was an argument and Viv's heart thundered as footsteps came in their direction. Three pursuers, she realised, two more than her captor could fight off. The men passed their hiding place, and came back, then their steps dwindled into the distance.

Her attacker remained motionless and Viv sucked in air around his hand. Now her pursuers had gone, she could focus on him. She had no idea why he had attacked her on the way to Esh-accom, loitered on Esh-accom's streets the night she arrived, or intervened now. Nor did she know his connection to the man in the cave who had aided Poss.

The rain flashed silver, which told Viv dawn was close, and the man's voice was suddenly harsh in her ear. 'You'll stay silent, elddra, unless you'd like to re-join your *friends* and for all my failings, I'm preferable to *them*. We're going to my lodgings where we need to speak, then you can go on your way, *after* certain undertakings. Do you understand?'

Viv nodded. She should have been reassured by her previous dealings with him but the rats of violent memories were free and she started to shake. He transferred his grip to her wrist, eased the gate open, and peered up and down. Then he stepped out, closed the gate silently behind them and continued up the alleyway, not going far before he entered a second compound. He had used the word *lodgings*, so Viv deduced the compound was not his.

He led her into the building and turned left down a passageway. The layout seemed the same as the arsehole's, which was handy if she wanted to leave without the man's permission, but when he pushed her into a room and locked the door behind them she saw the shutters were bolted too.

Chapter 14

Ky surveyed the shelves in frustration. How could the shelves behind him be crammed with scrolls and the ones in front be totally empty? He had seen the occasional empty shelf in the Bokos but this was different. Perhaps those who ordered the shelves had used some strange system only they knew about, or more disturbingly, perhaps the scrolls had been removed *or* destroyed. It would be a grave act to obliterate the thoughts of angels who had transcended *unless* they posed some sort of threat.

He had enough scrolls to occupy him for eons but the expanse of empty shelves troubled him and he set off back the way he had come. He counted his steps and turned where he must but remained preoccupied. As he walked, he wondered whether the Bokos, like the Halls and Haven, had been gifted to Ezam in its entirety. The Halls and Haven had beds, chairs, mirrors, baths and warm water to fill them, so perhaps the Bokos had come into being with all the shelves it would ever need. It was certainly a more palatable explanation than angel lore having been erased.

He arrived back at his usual work table, four thousand and five hundred steps later, and poured himself a draught of ambrosia. The honeyed-fluid should have soothed him but he paced about the small space. The scrolls he had collected lay ready but he felt too restless to study them and stared out the window instead. The view showed glis bronzed by the umber sky, loops of bright vines, and a forest floor adrift with leaves. The leaves fell, but never the glis, which remained as unchanging as Ezam's Hollow Hills, lakes, and Thorny Mountains.

For the first time in his eons of existence, Ezam's constancy felt stultifying rather than comforting. The Helixai changed, he reminded himself, but it seemed few angels had experienced it, or at least, spoken or written of it.

His thoughts turned reluctantly to Ash's description of the Green Helixai's transformation from gleaming green stone, to a place rank with blood and growth, back to gleaming green stone. Ash was the only blue angel in Ezam, but the mysterious Senquar-archae had been blue too. Had the Helixai changed in Senquar-archae's time ? And had its changes cost him his life, as Ash believed? And more troublingly, what had become of the angels who had blinked into existence with him? And most troubling of all, if events *were* to repeat, as Prime-archae Serith's obscure utterances suggested, what were his and Thris's fates?

Ezam's sky had cycled to peach before Ky headed back into the Bokos's dim centre. He counted his steps but took turnings on a whim, although he was careful to memorise these too. He nodded to the occasional Prime-archae bent over scrolls on the floor, or who wedged past him, arms laden, but eventually found himself alone.

It was hard to believe he was the only angel who ventured deeply into the Bokos. His fellow scholars might follow other passageways, he supposed, but it was odd he never came across them and he wondered if they lacked his counting and memorisation skills and feared becoming lost.

He went on, his thoughts on Senquar-archae's mysterious companions once more, and then the heavily stacked shelves gave way to empty ones at precisely four thousand, five hundred steps. His heart thudded. The same number as when he had first discovered the empty shelves via a *different* route.

He waited for his breathing to steady before he started back, worried suddenly his agitation might blur his memory and leave him marooned deep in the Bokos's labyrinth, but he arrived back at his usual table, four thousand five hundred steps later.

Ky slumped onto his chair and emptied several goblets of ambrosia. The glis still gleamed under a peach-coloured sky but everything else had been tipped on its head. He hoped for Prime-archae Mirek's company or even that of the abstruse Prime-archae Serith, but he remained alone.

He knew what he must do but poured himself another goblet of ambrosia and sipped it slowly, but in the end, this goblet was empty too, and he set out in a direction he had never taken before. He counted steadily but his agitation grew until it resembled that of his time with Thris in the lily-strewn water rift.

He passed four thousand steps and clenched his shaking hands to still them. Four thousand, four hundred; the shelves still groaned under eons of scrolls. Four thousand, four hundred and fifty; he could still be anywhere in the Bokos, and then, as he completed the last fifty steps, the dim outlines of stacked scrolls gave way to nothing.

He did not linger, knowing there would be time enough later to confront what he had discovered, just concentrated on the route back until he emerged into the small space next to the window again. 'Four thousand, five hundred steps, no matter which way I go,' he muttered.

'Or nine thousand steps in total,' said Prime-archae Serith, stepping from behind a shelf and settling on a chair. 'Nine is an interesting number, Kydane, in all its combinations,' he mused.

'In what way, Prime-archae?' asked Ky uneasily.

'Three is auspicious in many folds, and nine is three times three, which is the trinity of trinities,' he murmured, his gaze was on the glis beyond the window. 'Ashdane, Thrisdane, and Kydane; Senquar-archae, Anasdane and Paendane. We are missing a third threesome, Kydane, to make our trinity of trinities.' His purple eyes settled on Ky. 'Perhaps they went before; perhaps they are still to come; perhaps they are elsewhere in the Rynth.'

Kydane took a steadying breath. 'I have found something disturbing in the Bokos, Prime-archae.'

'All things in the Bokos are disturbing,' said Serith. 'The Bokos is circular, unlike the Halls and Haven. Nothing may hide in its corners. All things must be brought forth, willingly or unwillingly.'

The Prime-archae made angel lore sound like the creatures of Beast Fold but Ky pressed on. 'If I walk four thousand, five hundred steps in three different directions from this table, I reach a place empty of scrolls.'

'But not of angel lore.'

'There is nothing there,' said Ky in frustration.

'Which is instructive in itself.'

'Instructive? Of what do we speak?' asked Prime-archae Mirek, appearing juggling a scroll, a jug of ambrosia, and several goblets. He rested the scroll against the wall, filled the goblets, and listened while Ky recounted his experiences.

'Ezam is highly symmetrical,' said Mirek thoughtfully. 'It is not surprising a circular building has at its heart, a circular space. What did you *feel* when you were there, Kydane?'

'Dread,' admitted Ky.

'Why?'

'I wondered whether the angel lore had been removed.'

'Or destroyed?' asked Mirek, and Ky nodded.

'The blue angel Ashdane has the plumage of a Principae but remains manifest,' murmured Serith, gazing into space.

'And the heart of the Bokos is empty of angel lore,' added Mirek, then smiled reassuringly. 'Some mysteries remain beyond us but we must still strive to solve them.' He retrieved the scroll propped against the wall and unrolled it on the table. 'I have found a reference to Anasdane,' he said.

'The Dane who appeared with Senquar-archae,' said Ky excitedly, peering at the scroll.

'With *Sendane*, as he was then,' corrected Mirek, '*and* with Paendane.'

'So, did Anasdane and Paendane remained Dane?' asked Ky eagerly.

'The scroll speaks only of Anasdane spending much time in the rifts,' said Mirek as he carefully smoothed the parchment. *Anasdane described folds of floating plant caste, and those of endless water,* read Mirek. *He described how the water rose in great waves, to break upon the land, draw back, and break again. There were folds filled with danger that he visited only at his Archae's request.*

'His *Archae's* request?' whispered Ky. 'He had a mentor?'

'It would be a reasonable conclusion,' said Mirek.

Ky stared down at the table as he considered the mentor he had not seen since his return from Maze Fold. The Archae had not summoned him but Ky knew the fault lay with him. He no longer wanted a mentor, or at least, a mentor such as Archae Dejon but the prerogative to end the mentorship was likely the Archae's, not a lowly Dane's.

'Lacewings are more beautiful than scarabs,' said Serith abruptly, his purple eyes intent on Ky. 'Their wings are larger and delicately veined. Their colours are translucent. A scarab has small, blunt wings and their amethyst is dull. That is their nature, but their natures do not make one *superior* to the other. So it is with the Host who are part of the uncountable possibilities of the Rynth, and the Rynth, in turn, just a mote made possible by the endless glory of the Great Beyond.'

Serith's words were enough for Ky to leave the promise of unread scrolls behind and set out for the Halls. He did not fully understand the Archae's meaning, but Serith reminded those around him of the Rynth's essence and left listeners to make sense of it for themselves.

The white marble of the Halls emerged from the glis, and the myriad colours of various levels of Archae who stood or reclined on cushions in debate under the portico. Despite the arrival and departure of Archae, the debates remained the same and Ky wondered why they never grew weary of the topics.

He detoured around them and his even pace took him up the Hall's uncounted stairs and along its vast passageways to Archae Dejon's rooms. He took a deep breath, knocked, and entered on Dejon's command, bowed low and palmed. The Archae considered him with eyes as hard as the surrounding marble and it was Ky who finally broke the silence. 'I beg your pardon, Archae, that I have not presented myself to you sooner.'

'It is the Principae's pardon you must beg *if* I am right to assume you have abandoned the task they assigned you.'

'I … I will transit to Crystal Fold immediately,' said Ky, appalled he had overlooked his obligations to them.

'Not *immediately*,' corrected Dejon. 'You will first explain your disobedience to me.' Ky looked at him blankly. 'Is your memory so poor, Dane? My specific instructions were to return the shekinah here.'

'I must beg your pardon again,' said Ky shakily, and dropped his head. 'I was undone by fear.'

'Look at me, Dane,' ordered Dejon, and Ky raised his head. 'The Principae test us *all*, in all manner of ways to ascertain our worthiness to ascend. You will return to the Rynth and resume your task of Shadow. Thrisdane has already returned there, obedient to the wishes of *his* mentor. You will locate the shekinah and immediately return her here, regardless of Thrisdane's views on the matter.'

Ky's face burned with shame. 'I am incapable,' he whispered.

Dejon rose from his seat. 'I did *not* favour a Dane who is *incapable*, Kydane, nor one who is wilful, nor one who wishes to delay his ascension for eons. You *will* return!' Dejon's purple eyes blazed but all Ky saw were the fierce eyes of the beastman, the glare of the foul-smelling, web-wings, and the blank orbs of the squat, long-armed creatures.

He staggered in shock and then a curious sense of calm settled over him, and he bowed and palmed. 'I beg your pardon for *all* my failures, Archae, and thank you for your guidance, which is at an end. I will now transit to Crystal Fold and beg the Principae's pardon too.'

Ky had no memory of his exit from the Halls or from Ezam. The next thing he knew he was the Principae's all-encompassing turquoise light and their probings like knives in his head, then their glittering meadows were replaced with the rift's iridescent swirl, and the chink of glis leave as he made his way back to the Bokos.

Prime-archaes Mirek and Serith were at the table where he had left them, although Ky had no idea how much time had elapsed and whether their positions were coincidental. Mirek's expression was welcoming but Serith's face unreadable as was usual.

'Prime-archae Serith and I have been engaged in a small debate,' said Mirek. 'Would you unbed your wings, Kydane?' Ky looked at the Prime-archae in mystification but did as he was bid. 'I concede, Serith,' said Mirek, then bowed and palmed. Ky's unease grew and Mirek smiled. 'Bring your wings forward, Kydane.'

Ky did so, and gasped. A scatter of white plumage sat amongst the gold. 'I do not understand,' he whispered.

'Which is why we search the Bokos,' said Mirek, and looked pointedly at the scrolls on the table. 'Bed your wings again, Kydane. We have work to do.'

Chapter 15

Viv hugged herself while the man added more wood to the smouldering fire. She was wet, cold, and her hands stung where she had lost skin in her fall. The man remained intent on the fire until it blazed, then brushed the ash from his hands and turned. 'Come and warm yourself, Viv,' he said.

She edged past him and held her hands to the flames. 'Use this,' he said and handed her a drying cloth then poured her a mug of milk. 'Semna's cold, I'm afraid, and I've no time to heat it, but it's better than nothing.' Viv towelled off her hair and face, and took the drink, reminding herself she was his prisoner not his guest as he pulled two chairs to the fire. 'Take a seat, we need to talk.'

The man shared the same dark hair and brows as the man in the cave, but his hair was dark brown, not rusty, and he was far more self-assured. 'Well, you certainly stay true to type,' he said after a moment. 'You released the Waradi's Lefer and now the traders'. Not the way to make friends.'

Viv said nothing, and he drained his mug and set it down on the hearth. 'We don't seem to meet under the best of circumstances either, but this time, I think I did you a favour, Viv.' She had not told him her name but he could have discovered it by asking around *or* from the man in the cave. 'And are you wondering why I intervened?' he continued.

'I am guessing you want me to deliver a message to the *arse*—to the Syld,' she said.

'That's true, although I'm not a believer in mistreating wild creatures either.' He picked up his mug, went back to the table, and refilled it. 'I know your name but haven't granted you the courtesy of mine. I am Quen en-Sar-ril. The Sar Rill is in Genessavale,' he added when Viv did not react. 'And you're probably wondering why I'm so far from home.'

Viv was actually wondering where Genessavale was and whose side they were on. 'I'm not a good messenger,' she said to break the silence. 'The Syld hates and distrusts me. He believes I'm lein-trysted to a Waradi.'

'Because of the bracelet?'

Viv nodded. 'He ignored your kinsman's message and it didn't help I couldn't tell him who it was from. He'll probably ignore yours too. Why don't you deliver it yourself? Or give it to Sehereden. He'll pass it on.'

'It's too soon. The Genessi need to know the Eshadi's loyalties first. Esh-accom's Sylds seem content to do nothing, regardless of what happens in the vals, but Ataghan en-Scinta-ril seems different, and the val's Sylds look to him.'

'He's massacred Waradi *and* Ascadi if that's what you mean.'

'I've heard those of his own sett were murdered.'

'Murdering others won't bring his own people back,' she retorted and glanced at the window. The shutters blocked the light but dawn must be near. 'I need to get back or they'll come looking for me.'

'Given the Syld *hates and distrusts you*, that seems unlikely.'

'Not him, Sehereden, *if* he's returned.'

'Yes, I'd heard that Sehereden en-Scinta-ril enjoys the favours of the elddra who resides in his lein's compound.'

'Don't believe everything you hear,' snapped Viv. 'What's the message you want me to deliver?'

111

Quen retrieved a small wooden cylinder from his pack and handed it to her. 'Ask him to destroy it afterwards.'

Viv was surprised writing existed given the traders used pictures to identify themselves. 'Do you want me to keep your identity secret?'

'The message tells him what he needs to know,' said Quen, which did not answer the question, but Viv nodded and thrust the cylinder into her pocket. Quen tossed on his cape and handed Viv a jacket. 'It'll hide who you are. Cover your hair too,' he added, passing her a scarf.

Viv tied it under her chin, donned the jacket, and pulled the collar up. It was many sizes too big and its bulk disguised her as the cape had. He eased the door open, scanned and led her soundlessly out of the building. He scanned the alleyway too, and they made their swiftly back to the street. The bleak dawn promised another bleak day which kept people indoors, and they saw no one, even in Axian.

'You don't need to come any further,' whispered Viv, as they started down the street to the arsehole's compound. 'Especially as you don't want contact.' Quen simply strode on which told her he knew exactly where the arsehole's compound was and did not stop until they were close to the gate. 'Thank you for your help,' she said and handed back the scarf and jacket.

'Keep Sehereden en-Scinta-ril close,' he said, ignoring her thanks. 'The traders will seek redress from Esh-accom's Sylds. They're not likely to get it, but they won't forget *or* forgive the elddra who robbed them of so much coin.'

Sehereden and the arsehole's mounts were in the stable and as their heads turned, Viv abandoned plans to enter through Poss's window. She eased her mud-caked boots off at the door and padded inside. Her trousers were covered in mud too, adding to the chill of her wet jacket and shirt.

She wanted a warm bath and a change of clothes, but her clothes were in Poss's room and the little girl slept, so she headed for the kitchen fire. It was just a dull pile of coals and she knelt on the hearth as close to it as possible. Like some muddy version of Cinderella, she concluded sourly, and just as welcome.

She tensed as the kitchen door opened to emit a blast of rainy air but it was Tormis with a sling of wood. His bristly brows rose, and Viv shuffled sideways to make room, too cold to quit the hearth altogether. 'You're up early, elddra,' he said, as he rebuilt the fire.

The state of her clothes made it obvious she had never been to bed, and his use of *elddra* added to her irritation. She did not go around calling people *Eshadi*. 'My name's Viv,' she said, 'which stands for Violet Iris Vacia. Violet's my mother's name too, but she calls herself Lettie. I'm here because I'm looking for her.'

'I thought you were here because of your lein,' said Tormis mildly.

'My lein knows why I'm here,' said Viv curtly. The wood took and Viv had to shuffle backwards to escape the heat.

'Word spreads easily in Esh-accom,' said Tormis, as he cranked himself upright, 'and while I've not heard of a woman called Lettie, I've heard of a disturbance in Soaich Square.' He busied himself folding the sling and glanced sideways at her. 'Thieving's nothing new here, especially at Fire Zadic. Coin flows and thieves follow, and to keep

113

that coin flowing, Esh-accom's Sylds make sure thieves regret ever having passed the wall.'

Viv was tempted to retort that freeing *stolen* creatures was not theft but knew she should be grateful to Tormis for his warning. It was yet another reason not to hang around. 'Best get out of those wet clothes,' said Tormis, as he stowed the sling beside the stove. 'There'll be hot water now and you don't want to sicken.'

'The elddra don't suffer as the Valen do,' said Viv bitterly.

'All things that live, suffer, including the Lefer. Go get yourself warm.'

Viv spent a long time soaking in the large bowl the Valen used as a bath. The water was hot, as Tormis had promised, and she had retrieved her pack without waking Poss. It held the clothes Ithreya had gifted her, a comb, the tryst-bracelet and the tribute-charm and chain that, along with the amè casque, were the most she had owned since her mother had left. It still was not much, which was just as well, given she would need to make a quick get-away that night. Tormis's warning had been clear, but so had his kindness, which she considered as she combed her hair with comb Ithreya had gifted her.

Kindness was not much talked about *or* sung about, unlike love, which was like kindness with all the bells and whistles of passion, obligations, demands, and guilt. Kindness was a gentler, more forgiving thing. Tahsin had been kind to her when the arsehole had dragged her in, scarred and Waradi-tainted, and Sehereden had been kind to her too, but the fact remained that one day Sehereden

114

would have to choose between her and his lein, and she already knew who he would choose.

As for Poss … Viv would not leave the fold without saying goodbye which meant she must pay the arsehole's compound a final visit, hopefully when things were calmer and Ithreya's bond with Sehereden more settled.

She washed out her muddy clothes and pulled the plug. Pipes had brought water to Tahsin's sett too, but then it had been carted from room to room. Here it came out of taps and disappeared down plugholes like at home. That home had been gone for over a year now, judging by the length of her hair, but immeasurably longer in terms of how much she had learned.

She would make a new home with her mother, she promised herself, as she made her way back to Poss's room, but she sounded like a child in a playground squabble: *you don't want me here, but I don't care. I've got a better place to go. So there*! In the meantime, she would wait for Thris in the one place this fold had made her feel welcome.

Chapter 16

Poss woke as Viv arranged her wet clothes over the chair-backs. 'Viv,' she said, sleepily, and reached for her. Viv perched on the bed but Poss insisted she get in and then snuggled into the crook of Viv's shoulder. 'You smell so nice,' she murmured, as her fingers playing with Viv's curls, and Viv's throat tightened as she kissed the top of her head.

'Mereya says today will be the last of the rain, then Ser can take us around more of Esh-accom. It will be fun, Viv. Then Fire Zadic will start, and the tournaments, and the festivities. Oh,' she said, and sat up. 'I didn't show you the clothes Sehereden traded for you. He got some for me, too.'

'You showed me,' said Viv, perched on her elbow as Poss rushed to the clothing chest.

'No, these are new ones for the festivities,' said Poss, retrieving two neatly folded piles, and pushing the shutters wide. The light showed short-sleeved, short-waisted jackets, which seemed to fit over shirts of transparent material, and knee-length skirts. The light glinted off the rich design of birds on Viv's clothes, worked in gold and emerald-green thread, and flowers on Poss's, picked out in silver and blue. Both sets had the usual wavy lines around the cuffs and hems.

'You still need some boots, Viv. Ser didn't know what size you were.' Poss stroked the clothes. 'Aren't they lovely?'

'Yes,' said Viv, but her gaze was on Poss. Her dark hair fell in a waterfall around a face that bore no resemblance to the arsehole's. Viv wondered why Poss's mother had

116

not left her daughter with her biological father, but maybe she had dispensed so many *gifts* during the festivities, she did not know who he was, not that it mattered. Unlike Viv, Poss had grown up surrounded by love.

'You're thinking of Thris again, aren't you?' said Poss.

'No,' said Viv, and forced a smile.

'Do you think he's going to find you?'

'Yes—no, I don't know.' Poss really did ask the worst questions. Viv *hoped* Thris would find her, but hope was a poor excuse for reality.

'It will be his misfortune if he's not here for the festivities,' said Poss loftily. 'You'll have many men seeking your favours then.'

'Lots of things to do before the festivities, like having breakfast,' said Viv, scrambling out of bed. Poss's implicit understanding of sex made her uncomfortable, and she wondered what the age of consent was. Certainly not ten!

Poss struggled into her clothes and darted for the door, her jacket half on. 'You've forgotten to comb your hair,' said Viv, feeling like a mother. Poss came back and Viv grinned at her expression. 'I'll do something special with it.'

Poss handed Viv her comb and Viv took sections of hair and made a plait that extended from Poss's forehead down her back, then secured the end with a gold ribbon. 'Da got it for me yesterday,' said Poss, and snatched up a hand mirror. 'Oh, it's so lovely, Viv,' she said, and gave a twirl.

'It's called a French plait,' said Viv, her thoughts on the arsehole's love for his daughter again.

'*Frenchplat*? Did your mother *frenchplat* your hair?'

117

'Not with these curls,' said Viv lightly, regretting her slip. *Still more transference*! 'Let's see what Mereya has for our breakfast.'

Poss grabbed her hand and pulled her out of the room, just as Sehereden and Ithreya emerged from Ithreya's room opposite. Viv forced a smile and cursed Poss's timing as Sehereden's dark eyes held hers, and he brushed against her in the confined space.

Ithreya gave Viv a quick hug. 'Thank Enda you're back. Galian said it was still light when he left you at Axian and I sent Tormis to look too. Where have you been?'

'I met some elddra who invited me to eat with them,' said Viv, as Poss tugged her along the passageway towards the smell of fresh retsen.

'In the Old Quarter?' asked Sehereden, as they took their seats at the hall's table. Viv nodded and concentrated on passing the plates. Mereya trusted Poss with the mugs but not the jug of fresh urrut-sa or platter of steaming retsen. Sehereden filled Viv's mug, and when she emptied it, filled it again, and offered her more retsen, then Mereya delivered a bowl of spicy meatballs and he put two on her plate.

'You're hungry this morning, Viv,' he said and Viv nodded. He knew she ate after being hurt but not that running for her life and being seized by a stranger had the same effect, and she avoided his eyes as she started on the meatballs.

'Your hair looks lovely this morning, Fariye' said Ithreya.

'Viv did it,' said Poss, preening. 'It's called a *frenchplat*.'

The outside door slammed and Viv heard the arsehole stride up the passageway. He was either in a very big hurry or extremely angry. The latter, concluded Viv, as he stormed into the hall. He carried her cape, still covered in the mud from Soaich Square.

'Yours, I believe,' he said, his black eyes glaring at her, as he tossed it on a chair.

Poss had stopped in mid chew and Viv pushed her chair from the table. 'It's actually yours, Syld, from your compound, and I beg your pardon for not taking better care of it,' she said and snatched it up. 'I'll wash the mud off before it dries. I'll be back in a moment,' she said to Poss with a bright smile. She hurried off down the passageway, knowing the arsehole would follow to bawl her out, and that she would deliver the message cylinder and leave.

'The carving room, elddra,' he snarled behind her, and Viv continued past the washrooms. The carving room was not nearly as cheery without a fire and the arsehole threw open the shutters which added to the chill. 'Do you know what they do to thieves in Esh-accom?' he demanded.

'No.'

'They lash the men to poles in the middle of Axian and invite Esh-accom's citizens to beat them as they pass. They keep the women in cages in the same place. Their punishment is limited to curses and spit, and whatever the weather gods throw at them. The *only* reason you're not in that cage now, *elddra*, is because you're *my* guest.'

'I thought we agreed I wasn't.'

There was a burst of heat and Viv flinched. 'Don't bandy words with me, elddra! While you're in *my* compound, you—will—not—go—anywhere—near—Soaich—Square.' Each word was punctuated with a jab of his finger. 'Is—that—understood?'

He had been like this after the massacre and she wondered whether his night-time gallop had been to

119

retrieve drugs from his stash. 'I won't stand by and watch wild creatures being tortured.'

'They're none of your business!'

'That's what they said when they carted the Jews off to the gas chambers,' retorted Viv. '*Look the other way, keep your head down, it's nothing to do with you.* I won't do it even if you're happy to!'

'What in Soaich's name are you talking about?'

'I'm talking about right and wrong, something you know nothing about.'

His face was suddenly a hair's breadth from hers. 'I'll only say this once, *elddra*. Unless you give me your word to stay away from Soaich Square, I'll have you locked up here, for my daughter's sake, if not your own. Now, your word, *elddra*.'

'My word's worth nothing to you, arsehole, like me,' sneered Viv. 'But I'm going to solve your little problem for you. You won't have to put up with the embarrassment of an *elddra* in your compound for even another night, *or* in Esh-accom, for that matter. But I have something for you before I go.'

Viv pulled the message cylinder from her pocket. 'I'm playing messenger-boy again,' she said and handed it over. 'Not that it was much use last time.'

'Who gave you this?' he demanded.

'He said it would tell you what you needed to know,' said Viv and headed for the door. 'Oh, and you're to destroy it afterwards.'

'I haven't given you permission to leave, elddra!'

'No, you haven't, have you?' she retorted, and slammed the door behind her.

Viv left by Poss's window, and as she climbed out into the rain, she wished she had reclaimed the cape. She was going to very wet by the time she reached Tahsin's sett if she reached it. If the traders got their hands on her she would suffer something far worse than a public humiliation.

She reclaimed her boots, closed the gate soundlessly behind her, and hurried down the street. Her pack was slung over one shoulder and her jacket unbuttoned but the miserable weather was in her favour, and she only saw an occasional figure scurrying in the distance. Her hair darkened in the rain but her curls were a dead give-away. There seemed to be as few curly-haired people in the fold as red-haired ones.

She reached the wall and stopped in the lee of a building. The cobblestones gleamed wetly in the light, but the gate was closed and she had no idea whether she had to knock on a door somewhere to leave or whether she would be allowed. After what the arsehole said about the treatment of thieves, she might be on some sort of blacklist.

There were horses in the stables opposite and she slid deeper into the shadows. She had never worked out exactly who the horses communicated with or how close they had to be. The horses' heads swung towards the gate and Viv's skin pricked, then she heard the grind of wagon wheels on the other side and the Wall Guards exchange shouts with the new arrivals. The gate creaked open to reveal half a dozen horsemen and several wagons, and as the wagons and horsemen rumbled and clattered in, Viv turned up her collar, fixed her gaze on the ground, and strode out.

No one challenged her and she was about twenty lengths up the rutted track when the gate thunked shut behind her. The Wall Guards must have seen her but she guessed Esh-accom's Sylds were more interested in arrivals to their settlement *and* their tributes than those who departed.

The valley was broad, with the Eshacade a slice of silver away to her left and the dark edge of a forest in the distance to her right. Viv turned off the track and broke into a jog, heading for the forest and keen to get out of sight. The tussocky ground was rough, but running took her mind of Poss. She just hoped the little girl remembered Viv's promise not to leave *permanently* without a final farewell.

Chapter 17

Ataghan was still considering the message, when Sehereden appeared. 'Your daughter wonders where her lein is,' he said, with a smile.

'Gone.'

The smile vanished. 'Gone? What do you mean?'

'*I'm going to solve your little problem for you. You won't have to put up with the embarrassment of an elddra in your compound for even another night, or in Esh-accom,*' he mimicked.

'What problem?'

Ataghan prowled to the window. 'I was summoned to the Axian Compound this morning to collect my property.' He gestured to the cape. 'It was lost last night at Soaich Square by the thief who released two *amazing and exotic creatures* from their cages, and was delivered to the Axian Compound by the owners of those *creatures*, who not only identified the thief and demanded the usual punishment, but compensation as well.' Ataghan smiled sourly. 'As I bring a *lot* more coin into Esh-accom's coffers than the traders, they're now beyond the gates and the elddra remains uncaged.'

'But not safe! I need to go!'

Ataghan's hand fastened on his arm. 'Stay, Sehereden!'

'I won't have her put at risk. She's endured too much already.'

'She's at greater risk here, lein! I can't protect her again if she repeats the episode and there's no guarantee she won't!' Ataghan softened his voice. 'She's elddra, Sehereden, let her go. The elddra don't gift children and

Enda smiles on you with Ithreya. Don't risk Ithreya's gift by chasing after something that will gift you nothing.'

'Perhaps Enda smiles on *you*, lien, by sending us Viv,' said Sehereden. 'It's because of *her* you have Fariye, it's because of *her* Fariye has a lein to fill the void left by those of Esh-embrin. I've had more time with Viv, than you, lein. She's not like other elddra, even the elddra admit that. Nothing in her life's been easy or safe. Those who should have loved and protected her, did not.'

Ataghan's eyes flashed. 'The elddra love only their masters in the city of ice!'

'Viv loves Fariye.'

'She's made no secret of her intention to leave,' said Ataghan. '*If* she truly loved Fariye, she'd stay.'

'I'm confident she *will* stay and that, in the end, her love for Fariye *will* hold her here, as will the love of others,' he added softly. There was a short silence. 'And in the meantime, I intend to ensure she remains safe.'

'Before you do that, *lein*, read this.'

Sehereden looked at the message cylinder in mystification, then extracted the parchment and read. 'You've met this Genessi?'

'No.'

'Then how . . .'

'The elddra gave it to me, after she delivered her little speech. It seems she's had a busy night, between *liberating* Lefer and meeting with a man whose Vale has long ignored our slaughter.'

'She met with the elddra too,' said Sehereden thoughtfully. 'The ones I spoke with while you were in the Grey Fire.'

'The ones who knew nothing of her,' said Ataghan contemptuously.

'They knew more than they revealed, as I knew more than I revealed. But I did learn that at eighteen, Viv's far younger than other elddra in the Vales; that Violet Iris Vacia isn't an elddra name; and that elddra travel with a companion, and that, at least, fits.'

'The stinking Waradi leader,' spat Ataghan.

'I believe her contact with him was forced,' said Sehereden quietly. 'I meant Thris.'

'Thris?'

'Didn't Fariye tell you about him?'

'Fariye met this man?'

'No. Viv told Fariye they'd been separated in the fighting, and she told *me* she searched for him, as well as for her mother. From what she said, I believe they're lovers, another thing the elddra dismissed. Apparently, we cannot meet their needs.'

Ataghan's lip curled and Sehereden handed him back the scroll. 'When do we meet with this man?'

'*I'll* meet with him tonight. We'll draw attention if we both go.'

'Not something he wants,' said Sehereden.

'No. He lacks faith in Esh-accom's Sylds.'

'Don't we all,' muttered Sehereden.

Viv had no idea how late it was before she reached the trees. Sheets of iron-grey clouds hid the sun and a fine mist turned land into sky. On the upside, she saw no one, probably because anyone with any brains was snug in their compounds but on the downside, her jacket was soaked by the rain and her boots and trousers by the undergrowth. She half considered crawling under a bush to wait out the light, but it was warmer to keep moving.

She would take to the air as soon as it was dark and should be at Tahsin's sett before dawn. *And then what, Vivi? Ya goin' to spend ya whole life waitin' for ya angel man to show up?* Rim had always smashed her hopes and it was no different now. She *would* wait at Tahsin's sett but not forever. There would come a time when she must give Poss one last hug and leave, but that time was not now. *Now* she had to work out how to find Tahsin's sett from the air *and* in the dark. Viv's mouth twisted. It would be convenient if the new constellation popped into the sky tonight to light the way but given her luck, she was not holding her breath.

Her wet curls flopped in her eyes and she shook her head in irritation. If there were scissors *anywhere* in Tahsin's sett, she would cut her hair *really* short, *if* she ever found Tahsin's sett. Her best bet was actually to fly to Amethen's sett first, which was simpler to find given it was more or less straight north or *cloudwise*, and use smoke or lights to guide her the rest of the way. Tahsin's sett was small but there was always a fire burning somewhere, and some light should be visible *if* she flew low enough. But the strategy had obvious dangers, like becoming some bastard's caged *entertainment*.

It was hard going in the undergrowth and she stopped and sleeved her face. Anybody mad enough to travel in this weather would stay on the flatter land near the Eshacade, she realised, which meant she could probably fly with very little risk.

Getting airborne was always easier in clearings but the forest's edge also made it easier to be seen and Viv climbed what she hoped was one of the taller trees, intending to launch into the clear air at the top. But when she reached its crown, it was surrounded by even taller trees which meant she must launch vertically, which was harder.

She had done it before, she reassured herself, when pursued by the red-crested bully, but she had not flown since she had dragged the arsehole from the icestone pit and a practice flap would be handy. She unbedded her wings but the surrounding branches were too close even to spread them and she swore.

What ya waitin' for, Vivi? Scared, are ya? Rim's voice goaded her and she took a deep breath and leapt. Her wing clipped a branch and she was flung sideways, flapped madly to right herself, then cleared the trees and forgot everything but the thrill of flying.

God how she had missed it! The stream of cool, wet air over her skin; the rush of wind through her hair, the power and the freedom. She was beyond the sneering judgements of those on the ground and flew faster and faster, intoxicated by the blur of branches beneath.

She flew straight cloudwise, then recalled their party had crossed a ridge at some point after leaving Amethen's sett, *and* some rills. They had also ridden beside a rill for a time but she had no memory of any forest south of the sett and she had an awful feeling her speed had taken her too far north.

She swore again and turned back and frustrated by the darkness and canopy that obscured any rills, decided to land to orientate herself. She descended, found a small gap in the trees, and slid through but her wing snagged a bush as she landed and she was thrown forward onto her face. As much fun as exiting a rift, she thought acidly, as she spat the pungent leaf litter from her mouth, and then she heard voices.

Fear bedded her wings in an instant and she remained motionless, horribly aware of her blue clothes against

127

green. She was also close to the forest's edge but thankfully there were bushes between her and the more open ground.

The voices drew nearer and she hoped they were simply travelers from some sett on their way to Esh-accom for the festivities, but there was something about their intonation that made her stomach churn. *I own you, lein-tryst, remember that.*

They were close enough for Viv to feel the thump of the horses which told her the group was large and that they headed south. They might have already carried out an attack but there was no urgency in their travel and while Viv did not know the direction of the Waradi's Vale, it sure as hell was not south like Esh-accom.

The most obvious explanation was that they *planned* an attack. Viv had not seen any settlements in her flight but she had flown above the trees which hid the ground. Her breath hissed between her teeth. The last thing she needed was this sort of complication and even if she flew back and told the arsehole, what was she to say? *There's going to be an attack on a sett at least a day's ride from here, and yes I know I've only been gone half a day, and no, I have no idea which settlement.*

Maybe she should just keep going and forget she had seen anything. *Yeah, Vivi, it's nothin' to do with ya, is it? Just look the other way while those train-loads of Jews trundle on past to the gas chambers.* She had to go back. Even if it all ended in a crap heap, she had to try. She would fly as far as she dared, then run, and if the arsehole ignored her warning, then whatever happened would be *his* fault not hers.

She climbed the nearest tree, the provider of the pungent leaf litter, and scanned. The Waradi probably hugged the forest's margin for cover but she would put more distance between her and the forests' edge to be on the safe side. Her launch was more successful this time, thanks to the narrower crowns of the surrounding trees, and her flight back fueled by a fear of being too late to stop another Esh-embrin. She flew faster than she had ever flown before, and when Esh-accom's walls appeared in the distance, she landed and ran.

Chapter 18

The rain-softened ground was hard going and she cut across to the track which turned out to be not much better. There had been a lot of traffic into Esh-accom and muddy water added to the grime from her crash-landing while sweat added to the rain on her face.

She concentrated on the lope Thris had taught her but she'd had little exercise since being in Esh-accom and distracted herself from her burning lungs by concocting stories to explain how she knew of an impending attack *if* there was to be one. Each tale sounded more preposterous than the last and her angel part prevented her telling them anyway.

A horseman headed her way and Viv unbuttoned her jacket, prepared to fly away in full view of the wall if she must. The horseman slowed and she tensed as the gap narrowed then hissed in relief. It was Sehereden.

'Viv!' he exclaimed in relief, then took in her state. 'What's happened?'

'I need to … get back … to Esh-accom,' she said as she sucked in air. 'There's … going to be … another attack.'

Sehereden was suddenly on the ground beside her. 'Where? How do you know?'

'We need to get … back. There's not much … time.'

Sehereden leapt back onto Fara and hefted her up behind him. He asked no more questions which was just as well as Viv used all her strength to hang on. Sehereden did not slow even as they neared the gate, just bawled something to the Wall Guards, and as the gate swung open, swept through, across the yard, and up through the streets.

Luckily the weather kept people inside, thought Viv, as they swerved around corners.

Sehereden thrust the gate of the arsehole's compound open, leapt off, and strode inside, taking her with him but Viv still had no idea what she was to say. The arsehole was in the hall in conversation with Tormis but turned at their approach. 'I thought you were going to *solve my little problem* for me, elddra,' he said sarcastically.

'Viv says there's going to be another attack,' said Sehereden hurriedly.

'Where?' the arsehole demanded.

'I don't know. I don't know your lands. I heard a party of Waradi coming this way.'

'Coming *this* way? You're telling me they're going to attack Esh-accom?'

'No. I was a long way up the val. I heard them pass.'

'There's Esh-telin,' said Sehereden quickly, 'and Esh-mora, but that's further nightwise.'

'And they're both a day's ride from here,' said the arsehole. 'You can't have been anywhere near either place, elddra. The only thing you've heard is a Waradi plan to draw us into an ambush.'

'Believe what you want, arsehole,' retorted Viv. 'I had the choice to keep going or to come back and warn you. It's up to you whether you want another Esh-embrin!'

His eyes blazed but Sehereden broke in quickly. 'You said you *heard* them, Viv. Where were you?'

'In the trees. When I left here, I followed the forest up.'

'What were the trees like?'

'Different. Slender with a strong smell.'

'Syanwoods,' said Sehereden, his gaze flicking to the arsehole. 'Cloudwise of Esh-telin.'

131

'And a full day's ride away!' the arsehole retorted, and took several quick paces around the hall. Sehereden and Tormis watched him in silence, but Viv's gaze strayed to the jug of urrut-sa. She was thirsty, wet, and cold, now she had stopped running.

The arsehole swung back so suddenly she jumped. 'Send out word, Tormis,' he snapped. 'We leave as soon as I've twenty men.' Tormis hurried out and the arsehole's glare settled on Viv. 'You'll come too, elddra, to guide us to this place *a day's ride away* you reached in a quarter of that time *on foot*. And if you've betrayed us, you won't be coming back.'

Viv only had time to don a cape and down a mug of urrut-sa before she was back on Fara and heading down Esh-accom's streets. The pace was slower this time but the tension higher. Sehereden held his silence, as well he might. What the arsehole said was true. She could not have reached where she described, on foot, in the time she claimed, and that meant she lied, and if she had lied about this, she had lied about everything else. Viv gritted her teeth. If the price of stopping another Esh-embrin was to be Sehereden's trust, then so be it, but it still made her sick to the stomach.

There were a lot more than twenty riders at the gate when they arrived, in fact, Viv estimated there were closer to forty. 'Many follow my lein,' said Sehereden proudly, which was just as well, thought Viv, given what lay ahead.

She had plenty of time to consider Esh-embrin's charred corpses, the arsehole's ruthless massacre, and Sehereden's knifing of the Waradi leader as they rode. She dreaded the violence to come and hoped Esh-telin was

132

safely going about its business. To be called a liar was better than fronting a smouldering ruin any day.

The arsehole led, with his band members on the flanks and the others, including her and Sehereden, directly behind. His men knew how he operated and would pass on his commands to the rest of the group. She was confident the arsehole would win any fight, which given he protected women, children and the old, was a good thing, but she still found his ruthlessness repugnant.

The troupe followed the Eshacade, then turned along a rill that joined it sunwise. Normally Sehereden would have told her its name but the only sound was the pound of their mounts' hoofs over wet ground. The rain dwindled but the leaden clouds promised more. A second rill flowed in sunwise and again the group turned along its banks, the flatter ground quickening their pace.

The day drew on and as the light ebbed, the rain returned in icy squalls, full in their faces. The horses lowered their heads but all the men could do was pull their hoods forward. Sehereden's back protected Viv from the worst of it and she hoped the men did not know she was responsible for the excursion.

The forest loomed from the gloom to their right, and as the narrow bank forced them into pairs, Sehereden came level with the arsehole. 'A good place for an ambush, elddra,' he said, and Viv tensed as she realised the Waradi might have finished their murderous work and be lying in wait. There was a murmur as messages were passed between the men and the flick of the horses' ears told her they communicated too.

The bank narrowed further as the rill deepened, and they rode in single file. Fast-flowing water to their left, and a forest to their right. Viv wiped her sweaty hands on her trousers.

'The Telin Rill's swollen by Vorash,' said Sehereden, speaking for the first time. 'Esh-telin's close.'

There was no smell of smoke, but the rain would have washed the stench away. The bank widened again, then opened into a clearing, and Viv glimpsed the glow of lamplight over Sehereden's shoulder, and the dark outline of a sett. Esh-telin was intact and peaceful, and her breath emptied.

There was a challenge, and the troupe stopped as a lamp swung from the darkness, then the arsehole rode forward and spoke with its owner. The gist seemed to be that the sett's leader, along with many of Esh-telin's men, were at Esh-accom for the festivities, and that it was a perfectly normal night.

An invitation was extended to escape the Vorash's foul weather, which the arsehole accepted, and the rest of the men rode in. 'Ensure the horses are watered,' the arsehole said, bringing his mount alongside Sehereden's, 'and the men eat. No semna.' Sehereden nodded, and the arsehole's hand fastened on her wrist. 'The elddra and I are going on a little reconnoitre.'

He wrenched her sideways onto his horse, and as they continued up the track, Viv unbuttoned her jacket. She did not think the arsehole's threat, that she would not be coming back if she betrayed them, meant being dumped in one of the vals, and she searched the ground for a place to fly from.

He searched the ground too. 'Esh-telin's untouched and there's been no ambush. Is it to happen later, elddra?'

'I'm glad Esh-telin's safe, even if it gives you an excuse to kill me.'

'Kill you?'

'You've had two goes at it already, so third time lucky, eh arsehole? Why not do it now? Arrange an unfortunate accident so you'll have your lein all to yourself?' There was a burst of heat and Viv leapt off and scrambled up the slope.

He joined her on the ground but made no move towards her. 'You're wrong about me,' he said.

'I don't think so.' Her pack hit the ground, followed by the cape.

'What in Enda's name are you doing?'

'Making it easier to quit your company.'

'And join your friends the Waradi?'

The rain had stopped but the darkness hid his face and made it easier to speak. 'You're wrong about me,' she said, mimicking his earlier claim. 'Poss and I were close to Esh-accom when the Waradi caught us. She had been such a brave little girl, but I got careless. I should have kept to the trees, not to the rill where there was no cover. I hid her and ran, but I was never going to outrun horses. He caught me in the rill, pulled me up the bank, and smashed my head against the stone. He didn't knock me out, I wish he had. I felt everything he did to me. I can *still* feel everything he did to me.'

There was a long silence. 'That doesn't explain your behavior since nor your lies.' It was the first time he had spoken to her without anger or contempt. Maybe he found it easier to speak to the darkness too.

'I don't lie,' said Viv.

'It's not possible to reach Esh-telin on foot in the time you claim.'

'I reached *cloudwise* of Esh-telin *if* that's where the syanwoods are. We need to check there.'

135

'Because that's where the ambush is?'

His contempt was back and Viv sighed. 'I don't know what the Waradi intend, but they headed this way and they weren't in a hurry. Maybe they turned off to another sett.'

'And headed in the opposite direction to safety? Warinavale's sunwise, elddra, not nightwise!'

'But isn't Esh-mora that way? Maybe they decided to go there first.'

'And maybe you've decided to tell more lies.'

'Have it your own way, arsehole,' muttered Viv, retrieving her cape and slinging her pack over her shoulder. 'I'll check on my own.'

She set off along the bank, aware he followed on foot, and could end her life with a single knife-throw. The rain stopped and the cloud shredded, but it did not make the trudge any easier. She searched the forest for slender trees, and did not notice the swathe of churned earth until she heard the arsehole swear.

It appeared from the gloom ahead, angled sharply in front of them, and swept down to the rill. The rill's bed was broader here and the water shallower which made for a natural crossing place and, judging by the muddy tracks, a lot of horses had used it.

It could be Eshadi on their way to Esh-accom's festivities, she supposed, but the arsehole kept walking until he found dung, crouched and then sniffed the air. 'Stinking Waradi,' he spat.

'Can we catch them?'

'Too much of a start.'

He stared up at the sky, his silhouette so like Rim's, she looked away. Then he strode back the way they had come, gave a low whistle, and when the shadowy form of his horse appeared, leapt on. Viv thought he would ride away and leave her there but he wordlessly hefted her on behind.

The horse seemed eager to join its comrades and the arsehole let it have its head, Viv's heart in her mouth as it thundered through the dark and wet, but they arrived at Esh-telin unscathed. The arsehole leapt off, lifted her down and whispered something to his mount, then strode into the sett.

Chapter 19

The men were crowded in the hall which was deliciously warm and filled with smell of roasted meat. The arsehole drew Sehereden aside and they spoke briefly before separating to speak with other men, who spoke with other men in turn. It was the way they had communicated on horseback, but it was odd they did so on the ground.

An elderly woman offered Viv urrut-sa, which she gratefully accepted, and sipped it as she watched the news spread of Esh-mora's likely fate. The men looked grim, which was unsurprising, but there was something else there too, familiar from her time in gangs. The static in the air before a storm or in the gang's case before a raid on a rival squat.

The arsehole's men slipped away so that soon only Esh-telin's men remained, along with Sehereden and the arsehole, who were clearly in charge. Older men hovered, as anxious as the grey-haired woman who had served Viv. There were no women and children though which probably meant they had been packed off to the most secure part of the sett.

The fire burned low and she yawned, weary from her flight, long run, and clinging on during the ride, but she did not think she would be offered a bed with a chocolate on the pillow. The rest of the men left and the arsehole followed them out, which left Sehereden, and there was no mistaking his coldness. He had trusted her against the odds in the past but even he could not swallow her claim she had been cloudwise of here earlier that day.

He beckoned her from across the room. 'You're to stay with me. Whatever orders I give, you're to obey immediately.'

Or else what, wondered Viv, as she followed him out into the chill air. She guessed they were to lay in wait for the Waradi, who the arsehole obviously expected to return, and she had the potential to blow everyone's cover. At least she was not bound and gagged, which meant there might be a skerrick of trust left, although the arsehole's orders might be to put a knife through her instead.

Sehereden gave a low whistle and Viv stared at the sky, clear for the first time in days. 'I'm not in league with the Waradi, Sehereden,' she said.

His eyes were on the sky too. 'You need to start making sense. There's a point beyond which trust becomes the act of a fool.'

He was right, but his words cut her to the core. She wanted to explain why she acted as she did, to show him she was a decent, honest, truthful person, worthy of *love*. But she was not a decent, honest, truthful person, worthy of love. She had thieved, and conned, and twisted words until they bore little resemblance to truth, and she had caused the death of a child.

And now she competed for a man another woman loved; a woman who could give him the child he desired *and* the truth, the very things Viv could never give him. And even while she yearned for his love, and the home he offered her, she yearned for Thris's love, and a home with her mother. The bitter truth was that having Sehereden had always been a fantasy, and what better time to end it than here and now, while they waited for another blood bath.

Fara appeared and Sehereden leapt on and hauled her up behind him. 'We're positioned in the forest. If the

Waradi *have* destroyed Esh-mora, they'll have to return this way to cross the Telin Rill, it's the only ford for many lengths cloud- and star-wise. They're likely aware of Esh-telin's existence but if not, they'll smell its smoke.'

And detour to add its destruction to their list of triumphs, deduced Viv. She hoped to God the women and children *were* in the safest part of the sett, although the arsehole probably planned that the Waradi never got anywhere near it. Plans did not always work out though, as her time with Thris had proved.

Fara continued past the ford and turned up the slope towards the forest. The ground was littered with rotten logs and as Fara stumbled, Viv grabbed Sehereden's jacket, sensed him recoil, and let go, his physical rejection of her another wound.

They entered the trees' deeper darkness and Sehereden brought Fara to a halt. Viv had no idea how many other men were secreted amongst the boles and what their part in the fighting would be or Sehereden's, for that matter. Was he to gallop down flinging knives, with her riding behind, or was he to off-load her? And how was he to prevent her aiding her Waradi *allies?*

'You won't be involved,' said Sehereden briefly, and Viv realised Fara had communicated her thoughts.

'I'm already involved.'

Sehereden made no response and as time stretched away, Viv's thoughts wandered, and then all hell broke loose. There were shouts and the pound of horses, and Sehereden urged Fara out of the trees and positioned him midway down the slope. Other riders appeared beside them to form a line between the rill and the forest. There was another line of men visible in the dimness ahead so the fighting she heard must be closer to the sett, and she realised the Waradi had been allowed to approach it, and been ambushed.

Waradi who escaped to gallop back towards the rill, would be cut down by the line of the arsehole's men in front, and any who escaped *them*, would be finished off by Sehereden's men. Viv gripped Sehereden's jacket, scarcely able to breathe, and then a riderless horse galloped from the darkness. The men created a gap to let it go and a second, *mounted* horse, followed, and swerved upslope as its Waradi rider saw them. He pounded past Sehereden and Viv, but as the men closed ranks, wrenched his horse back.

The slope was slick and it went down on its haunches and cannoned into Fara at speed. The shock hurled Fara sideways and Viv was aware of being airborne, and of hitting the ground. The world disintegrated and then burst back as pain exploded in her arm. She was aware that horses thumped about her, that men grunted as they fought, but then the sounds faded. The last thing she heard was the arsehole's voice and then there was nothing.

Ataghan came swiftly down the bank as he surveyed the battle's aftermath. Two dead Waradi, and no injuries to his men, except for Sehereden. At least he was back on his feet, just, as was Fara, though lame. The rest of the Waradi already formed a pyre back at the sett, as did three of his men, and there were several nasty slash wounds there like Sehereden's, in the process of being stitched by the sett's surgeon.

But his lein refused aid until he knew the elddra's fate and she still lay motionless. 'Does she live?' rasped Sehereden.

The men who held Sehereden upright said nothing but they waited and Ataghan's jaw clenched as he turned her. The dawn's cold light showed her eyes were closed, and that a bruise crept over her temple. She breathed but the pulse in her neck was erratic. 'She lives,' he said, but the blow to the head might soon put an end to that. He ran his hands lightly over her right arm, feeling for breaks, and then the left one, and froze.

'What is it?' demanded Sehereden, seeing his reaction.

Ataghan forced himself to look up, to meet Sehereden's eyes. 'It's a Soaich break,' he said and took a steadying breath. 'I'm sorry, lein.'

It was going to be a fine day, as the first day of Fire Zadic always was, the sky the same delicate blue as at the Scinta Rill and Ataghan looked at it often as he rode. He knew his sett had gone and those who had filled it, but his plans to rebuild it took his mind off the elddra he carried.

He was beyond weariness, as was Taris, but the big stallion did as Ataghan bid and took him swiftly to Esh-accom. Speed might save the elddra, or the surgeon who dwelt in Anaten Quarter, or even her elddra blood, but he doubted it. Those who suffered Soaich's breaks did not long escape Soaich's realm.

He had bound the arm to her side to prevent movement, but done nothing more. Once the bone was through the flesh, herbs that cured smaller hurts did more harm than good. He was grateful she remained unconscious, but her face had flushed with the fever Soaich sent to hurry his guests along.

His men followed more slowly with the wounded and Sehereden would not be back in Esh-accom till late that

142

night or early the next morning. It would be best if the elddra died before then, although there would still be the pyre to prepare, and Fariye to comfort, though only Enda knew how.

The Waradi dead were already ashes as were the dead who had rode out with him, but his band had escaped serious injury except from Sehereden, whose refusal to abandon the elddra had left him vulnerable. It had been a mistake to deny his lein's request to leave her in the sett's safety. He had mistakenly thought Sehereden's trust in her finally broken and had wanted the elddra to witness the results of her treachery.

His mouth hardened as he contemplated how the elddra teased the Waradi and Eshadi into conflict with each other, like a maragh sow teased a boar, and he considered the elddra's relationship with the Genessi. Perhaps it was *Quen en-Sar-ril* who was the source of her information about the Waradi's plans, but whatever its source, even Sehereden saw the impossibility of what the elddra claimed to have witnessed.

Ataghan had sent his band to investigate Esh-mora's fate and he suspected they now spent the day tending a pyre. At least the men, women, and children of Esh-telin slept safely in their beds, and the men who had ridden with him had tasted the sweetness of destroying those who had murdered their children. He would have no lack of willing workers to rebuild his sett and afterwards, to bring their trysts and children to live with him there.

The elddra was wrapped in her cape but as Ataghan neared the wall, he pulled his own cape over her too and then took the narrower back streets to avoid the crowds. To the casual observer, he simply carried a bundle of goods. Nor did he draw attention by going faster than a trot, which was fast enough given the fine day had drawn people into the streets. It was kinder to Taris too, who now went with his head down.

Ataghan reached his compound and pushed the gate open. Tormis swept magellus blossoms in the yard but dropped his broom and hastened to Taris's side. 'Syld?'

'I need Baraghan,' he said, as he slid from Taris's back, cradling the elddra.

Tormis hurried off, surprisingly fast for a man of his age, and Ataghan made his way inside. Mereya was cutting ardins for a stew, but tossed off her apron when he appeared with the elddra in his arms. 'See to Taris, will you?' he said, as he headed down the passageway. 'And I need a fire in my room.'

He kicked open the door and lay the elddra on the bed, pulled off her boots and untied the cloth that bound the broken arm to her side. He slid her sound arm out of her jacket, but her arm was free of the shirt sleeve which was knotted around her neck. He was too tired to feel surprised, just turned his attention to the broken arm.

He had seem some terrible injuries since the fighting's start but braced himself as he eased her left arm out of her jacket which was difficult, given the bone no longer gave the flesh shape, and he must avoid touching the bloodied ends that pierced the flesh.

The door opened and Mereya came in with a load of wood and stopped. 'Enda's grace! Oh, Syld,' she whispered, her gaze on the elddra. 'Tormis has gone for Baraghan?' Ataghan nodded, busy with the arm. 'Ithreya took Fari to her own compound early today to see the young ones there. The child's fretted all night for her lein.'

Ataghan nodded again and Mereya dumped her firewood on the hearth. 'Take yourself to the washrooms,

Syld. You're dead on your feet. I'll fetch you some clothes, get the fire going, and clean her up. It's all we can do until Baraghan gets here.' And after he leaves, we can prepare the pyre, thought Ataghan, but he kept the words to himself.

Chapter 20

The tub of hot water was so delicious Ataghan all but fell asleep but he hauled himself out, donned clean clothes, and forced himself back along the passageway. The door was ajar and he heard Baraghan's resonant voice. Mereya stood by the bed supporting the elddra's lower arm, while Baraghan wiped his hands with a pungent smelling cloth.

Ataghan had not seen him for a couple of zadicans but he looked the same: a head of dark reddish-brown hair, fair skin, and the deep blue eyes Valen women found irresistible regardless of other lovers or even trysts. It was fortunate Baraghan's fighting skills matched his healing ones.

'You never cease to surprise, Syld,' he said, as Ataghan came in. 'I'd heard you secreted an elddra here but not an Angellus.'

'Everyone knows the Angellus are long gone,' said Ataghan shortly. 'Is there anything to be done?' There was a jug of semna on the table and he poured himself a mug and gulped it down.

'There are always things to be *done*, Syld, whether they deliver the desired results is another question entirely.' He handed Ataghan the cloth. 'Clean your hands, Syld, and you can take over from Mereya. I'm sure she has other things to do.'

Ataghan wiped his hands and took the elddra's arm, and Baraghan waited for Mereya's footsteps to echo away before he spoke again. 'How did it happen?' he asked, as he unplugged a bottle of foul-smelling liquid, and dampened a second cloth.

'She came off a horse during a skirmish with the Waradi.'

'Where?'

'Esh-telin.'

'I heard you'd pulled men out of Esh-accom and headed cloudwise at speed, but Esh-telin's a fair ride. How did you know the Waradi were there?' Baraghan dabbed the bones with the cloth, but glanced up when Ataghan failed to answer. 'Oh, another case of *Mad At's* prescience.'

'Call it what you like.'

'I'd prefer to call it *what it is*. A liking for the truth is an unfortunate side-effect of my seed-father. Now, extend the limb. Gently does it. We don't want our beauty to end up with one arm longer than the other.' He lay the elddra's sound arm on the covers, examined the two critically, then dug his fingers into the wound and worked the bones.

Ataghan winced but Baraghan stared into the middle distance, then withdrew his bloody fingers. 'Keep her *absolutely* still,' he said, his ragged voice evidence of the effort it had cost him. He wiped his hands, pulled splints from his pack, and did not speak again until he had finished splinting, and had started to stitch. 'If she *were* elddra, she would be dead by now,' he said conversationally. 'I gather she went with you because of your lein?'

'Why do you gather that?'

'An *elddra* who keeps company with a Valen draws attention, but an *elddra* who looks like her …'

'She's my *daughter's* lein, not Sehereden's.'

'*Yet*,' said Baraghan.

Baraghan goaded him but Ataghan refused to bite. He had extricated Baraghan from some vicious fights in the past, and Baraghan had put Ataghan's band members back together when other surgeons had despaired, but they shared more than favours.

Baraghan finished stitching in silence then bound the wound. 'Hold her on her side. We need to ensure she keeps that arm still, especially once Soaich gets his claws into her.' Ataghan did as he was bid, but Baraghan paused to run his hand over her naked back.

'More broken bones?' asked Ataghan, cursing he had failed to check beyond the arm.

'A little experiment,' said Baraghan as he brought the bandage under her sound arm, and up and over her broken one. 'As you know, the Angellus are sometimes depicted as winged and sometimes not. The prevailing wisdom, *if you call it that*, is that only some Angellus were winged. I'm inclined to believe they were all winged, but had the facility to hide the fact.'

Ataghan snorted and Baraghan eyed him as he bandaged. 'I find it odd that while I *enjoyed* the Astraali's *hospitality* longer than you, your hatred is greater than mine. As a healer, I feel bound to warn you against its corrosive effects.'

'Which you purge through your extra-Fire Zadic activities,' sneered Ataghan.

'And you through your fighting.' The air frissoned and then Baraghan smiled. 'Hatred won't keep the elddra alive, Ataghan, in fact, it damages those of Angellus blood. The elddra's best chance of beating Soaich lies in love. She needs your lein.'

'He's somewhere between Esh-telin and here with twenty stitches in his shoulder.'

'Then your daughter.'

'Absent too, and I won't have her distressed.'

'Then you'll have to use what you've got. I'll demonstrate in case you've forgotten.' He smoothed the elddra's curls back and for a moment Ataghan thought he was going to kiss her but he gently breathed into her mouth, waited for her chest to fall, and delivered his breath again when she inhaled.

'You can help her live, Ataghan, but if your hatred is too great for the task, I'll take her with me.'

'I summonsed you,' Ataghan reminded him tersely.

'You did indeed, but be aware that *any* aid you offer will be useless once Soaich's fever really takes hold. She'll be on her own then and if she's still with us this time tomorrow, Enda can mark it up as one for him.' Baraghan snapped the lacings on his pack shut, and slung it over his shoulder. 'I'm off to see what wonderful creatures the wagoners have brought to *delight and amaze* us. It's probably some bedraggled Lefer, but I live in hope the Angellus have paid us another visit.'

'You're alone in that.'

Baraghan half smiled. 'Take care, Ataghan.'

Ataghan tossed more wood on the fire, even though it roared, and poured himself more semna. He sipped it as he wandered to the window and back to the bed. He had delivered hareesh to her, mouth to mouth, in the Grey Fire, and would deliver his breath, not that he must do so for long, her face was already filmed with sweat.

He locked the door, pulled a chair to the bed, and breathed into her mouth as Baraghan had, but caught her exhalation and heat seared through his body. He clenched his hands and delivered another breath, careful to turn his head aside this time. There was no sign his breath helped her but he knew it strengthened her for the fight ahead and continued his rhythmic delivery until the elddra gave a shuddering groan.

'So, it begins,' he muttered and gulped down the last of the semna. There was a knock and he opened the door to admit Mereya who bore gorash and a fresh jug of semna. 'Is there anything I can get the elddra, Syld?' she asked.

'She's fevered, Mereya. It's between Soaich and Enda now.'

'I can watch, if you wish, so you can get some rest.'

'She's of my compound,' said Ataghan briefly. Mereya nodded and he slumped onto the chair and hefted his feet onto a second one. Soaich took less than a day to do his work, depending on his victim's strength, but the elddra's blood might stretch it to two. He downed another mug of semna and felt it loosen his muscles enough to eat. He was not hungry but must eat to maintain his strength for the tournaments.

The bruise on the elddra's temple had faded to green, proof of the power of her elddra blood, but it would not be enough to beat Soaich. Ataghan grunted. He had never set great store by gods; the elddra's smashed arm had resulted from a clash between men, not Soaich and Enda.

Her breathing sank to a harsh panting and he prowled around the room, and then she muttered something and he returned to the bed. Her eyes were open, almost purple in the afternoon light, and Ataghan's guts tightened. 'What is it, elddra?' he asked, but whoever she stared at, it was not him.

No! Stop it. You're hurting her! Leave her alone! I hate you, I hate you, I hate you! It was a child's pleadings, eerily delivered in a child's voice, and Ataghan's jaw clenched. More muttering followed, too jumbled to follow, and then there was another burst of clarity. *Don't! Don't. Please. Please. Oh, God. Oh, God.* The voice had changed now, older but no less terrified, and its tone betrayed the type of violence done to her. *Oh God, oh God, oh God.* Then she sobbed, a harsh, dry sobbing and Ataghan went to the window and leaned out, knuckles white on the sill.

More incoherent mumbling followed, which he hoped signaled the end of the revelations, but then she repeated the word *rim*, over and over again. Ataghan had no idea whether it was a person or a thing, or why she said it with such love *and* hate. Her pillow was soaked but he was too jarred to ask Mereya for a fresh one.

Sehereden had told him the elddra had a violent past, but being told and hearing it from her own mouth were different things. She was quieter now but her eyes moved as if she watched something, and he checked whether a bird had flown in. There was nothing, but her gaze was so intense the hair shifted on the back of his neck.

Thris, come back to me. Come back to me, Thris. Come back, Thris. Thris, Thris. There was such longing in her voice, he winced. This was the man Sehereden had told him about, who had been with her before the fighting. But which fighting? And where was he now? Dead, most likely, as he had not returned.

Her muttering continued and then he heard the shrill pipe of Fariye's voice in the hall, and the patter of her footsteps up the passageway. A door opened opposite and closed again, as she discovered the elddra was not in her room, then there was a rat-tat-tat on his door. 'Da? Are you there? Da?'

He opened the door a crack and slid through into the passageway and she scrambled into his arms, as she always did when they had been apart. 'You're back!'

she squealed, and planted warm kisses all over his face. 'Is Viv with you? Is she back too?' Ithreya came up the passageway more slowly, her face telling him Mereya had passed on at least some of the news.

'Viv's been hurt, Fari,' said Ataghan gently. 'And Ser too.'

'Both?' asked Fariye, in a small voice. 'Was there fighting?'

'Yes.'

'Where are they now, da? I want to see them.'

'Sehereden is still on his way back. He needs to come slowly and then he will need to sleep. You can see him after that.'

'And Viv, da? Is she here?'

'In my room, Fari, but she's very sick.'

'I want to see her!'

Fariye twisted in his arms but Ataghan tightened his grip. 'No, Fariye.'

Fariye's dark eyes fastened on his. 'Is she dying?'

'Yes.'

Tears started down her cheeks .'Then I must be with her,' she said thickly.

'Fariye …'

'You told me leins are one,' she choked. 'If Ser were dying, you would be with him, wouldn't you, da?'

'Fariye …'

'Wouldn't you, da?'

There was a tingling silence but Ataghan had never lied to his daughter. 'Yes, I would be with him.'

He half opened the door but paused. Ithreya waited quietly, her face grim. 'My lein suffered a knife wound to the shoulder yesterday but there was a good surgeon in Esh-telin, and he'll heal, all the better if you care for him. He should be here late tonight or perhaps early on the morrow. When he arrives, you can reassure him I will have Fara retrieved from Esh-telin as soon as he is sound.'

'I will. Thank you, Syld,' said Ithreya.

Chapter 21

Fariye leapt from Ataghan's arms as soon as he entered the room, and scrambled onto the bed. 'Don't touch her arm!' he warned as Fariye crouched beside the elddra, and cradled her sweat-slicked face.

'You can't die, lein, because you promised before you left, you'd say a proper goodbye, and you haven't said one, so you *can't* go,' she said tremblingly. 'And you're my lein, and lein's don't leave each other. Leins hang on.' She took a choking breath. 'They *fight* to hang on, Viv, like you fought to keep me safe.'

Fariye dashed the tears from her eyes. 'Do you remember when you found me?' she asked, breath catching. 'Do you remember? I . . . I thought you were the bad men . . . but you sat in the dark with me . . . and you sang to me, and you let me sleep on your lap, and . . . and you carried me up and down the ridges, even when you were tired, so you can't leave now, lein, not when you're safe with us. Ser loves you, and I love you, and they'll be dances, and shallit.'

Fariye sobbed and Ataghan gritted his teeth. Fariye had seen too much death but she had a right to be with her lein.

'And after Fire Zadic . . . da and Ser will rebuild our sett on the Scinta Rill,' she said between sobs, 'and it's the best . . . the best sett in the whole of Eshavale. And when Thris comes back . . . he can be there too. So, you can't leave, lein, you can't leave. Thris won't know . . . he won't where to find you. You *have* to be here, lein. You *have* to stay with me, lein. I love you. I love you, lein. You *have* to stay. I love you, Viv, you *have* to stay. I love you, I love

154

you. Stay with me, Viv, stay with me.' Fariye collapsed against the elddra's neck and her pleas were so painful that he had to leave.

Ataghan exited his compound and strode off down the street, fighting the burn of his body. Had he been beyond the walls he would have galloped Taris until exhaustion claimed them both but he was confined to Esh-accom until after the festivities. Shadows striped the cobbles and he was surprised only a day had elapsed since his return.

Esh-accom was a place where he exchanged urrut hides and fleece for coin, competed in tournaments, won the gifts of women and the hope of a child that lasted all the way till Glimwing. It was not a place he ever wanted to call home.

The streets were narrow and the whole settlement hemmed in by a wall that he sourly concluded mirrored the imaginations of its Sylds. As long as the Waradi or Ascadi murderers were not actually at the gate, or worse, interrupted the flow of tributes, the Sylds were content.

Heat surged anew and he briefly considered turning back to his stables to take that gallop after all. Taris could gallop all day and jump the ridges, unlike Fara. If Sehereden had been on Taris at Esh-embrin, neither he nor the elddra would have been injured.

Ataghan strode on across Axian, now very different from its desolate emptiness of Vorash. The rinks had been set, the stalls already crowded with those eager to trade, and men were busy erecting the semna-firi tents. They would be in demand once the tournaments began, as would those at Enda's Grove in the Anaten Quarter.

The first evening of Fire Zadic always brought Esh-accom's multitude of visitors onto the streets, keen to sample everything on offer. The short, caped-figures of Stonash queued at shallit stalls alongside their kin the Long-arms, the plainly dressed Valen from far-flung vals, and the women whose finery told of setts with urrut herds in the hundreds.

Ataghan's keen gaze took in his likely competitors as theirs took in him and the lingering glances of women who might favour him followed him as he slid through the crowd. The air already held the faintest scent of atunement, but Ataghan did not break his stride. The scent would strengthen as Fire Zadic unfolded to feed the festivities and, if Enda were generous, to gift the seeding of children.

The crowds dwindled as he exited Axian into the Anaten Quarter. Brithergen and Ithreya's kin had compounds here but he did not seek them out. He wanted to clear his head and use up the last of the daylight, among other things. He chose a route through Esh-accom's more obscure streets to refresh his memory of its ways, and when its sunwise gate came into view, turned starwise, choosing streets at random but heading inexorably towards the Old Quarter.

Lamps of stained glass special to Fire Zadic, threw coloured mosaics onto the cobbles and the air filled with fragrance as he neared Enda's Grove. The Grove's gardens and flowering bushes were still quiet, and he continued to the Old Quarter and turned starwise again. The Genessi's message had been specific as to the meeting's time and place, but Esh-telin meant he was two days late and the Genessi may have departed.

Ataghan found the street and compound without difficulty and checked his knives as he entered the yard. The compound was quiet but his knock was answered swiftly, and he stepped into the room. Quen en-Sar-ril was tall, armed, and not averse to making his appraisal of Ataghan clear.

The table showed the remains of a meal and a full pack by the bed suggested the Genessi was about to leave, festivities or not. 'I regret I was unable to meet you as planned,' said Ataghan briefly.

'I heard you'd gone to Esh-telin to clean out some Waradi filth,' said Quen, shifting the plates from table to floor, and gesturing Ataghan to a chair. He filled mugs from a jug on the shelf, and handed Ataghan one. 'It's semna but lacking in anis and therefore lacking in taste, but I've heard that's how you like it here in Eshavale.'

Ataghan grunted and took a sip. 'If it's an alliance you seek, why not approach Esh-accom's Sylds?' he said without preamble. 'They influence the surrounding vals, especially along trade routes.'

'Because they appear to have a great deal in common with the Genessi Sylds of Gen-ardin and Gen-soril, whose interest lies only in trade, and so far, trade has not been affected,' replied Quen, equally blunt. 'The Waradi concentrate their attentions on the more cloudwise setts, like the one I once lived at.'

Ataghan took another sip of his drink. Quen was not much use to him if he were just a solitary Genessi intent on revenge. 'My lein killed the Waradi leader some time ago,' he said with a shrug.

'There are always more. You won't have heard of the Perin-ril but the Astraali have. There's a nest of their brood there, expelled from Astraal to make their mischief in the Vales.'

Ataghan straightened. 'How many?'

'Perhaps thirty.' Quen drained his semna and leaned forward over the table. 'Their sett is at the rill-head and the val's narrow. It's a natural trap *if* you hold the ridges. They won't expect an attack starwise *and* cloudwise. Together we could destroy them.'

'And the Ascadi?'

'Followers but not fools,' said Quen, easing back in his chair. 'They'll reconsider the wisdom of leaving their Vale if Perin-ril's annihilated.'

The Genessi made sense *if* he were to be trusted. 'What are your dealings with the elddra?' he asked.

Quen's eyebrows rose. 'The messenger you *hate and distrust*? Her words, not mine,' he added, as he refilled his mug and topped up Ataghan's. 'Violet Iris Vacia; the elddra who appears where no elddra ever treads, who does what no elddra ever does, who cares for things the elddra spurn. What *is* she really, Ataghan en-Scinta-ril?'

'You tell me.'

'My kinsmen came across her high in Warinavale while he carried out a reconnaissance that all but cost his life. It all but cost the elddra's life too, but for different reasons. She liberated some Lefer the Waradi were using for gaming and got slashed in the process. My kinsman would have got her away *and* himself, had it not been for a maragh.' He smiled sourly. 'It didn't help her trust that he was disguised as a Waradi.'

'And then?'

'She tried to rob him, in *your* Vale this time, where he had detoured to stay alive. She had a sick child with her and needed a mug to carry away his fire coals.' Quen laughed. 'You'd think an elddra would come up with a more convincing story, wouldn't you? The cave was full of oilstone.'

'He gave her the mug?'

'Yes, and aided the child, who I believe is your choose-daughter?'

'And sent them on their way?' asked Ataghan, ignoring Quen's question.

Quen nodded. 'In exchange for delivering a message.'

'*Enda lies nightwise,*'Ataghan tossed off.

'Obscure, I grant you, but all my kinsman could risk, given his predicament. He made it home but a clearer message needed to be delivered. It's taken me longer than I predicted, thanks to the Waradi and Ascadi that roam your vals, but I was just a few days out when I came across the elddra again.

He smiled dryly. 'She stumbled into *my* camp this time and I considered using her as a messenger then like my kinsman had, but needed time to acquaint myself with your reputation.'

'And once you had, why not approach me directly?'

'I intended to until I noticed the elddra alone in Esh-accom's streets. Between your lein and your choose-daughter, she's rarely without company. I followed her into the Old Quarter but she went off with other elddra before I could approach. The next time I saw her, she was being pursued by some very angry traders so I intervened. It also gave me the opportunity to charge her with my message.' Quen's brows drew. 'But given her description of your relationship, I'm surprised you came.'

'Most of what she says is lies but I have a particular interest in eliminating the Waradi.'

'If she's a liar, why have her in your compound?'

'She's lein to my daughter.'

'Ah, I see.'

Ataghan drained his semna and rose. 'There are matters I must attend to, but I would like to meet again. You'll be here tomorrow night?'

'One more night.'

Ataghan nodded. 'We'll speak then.'

Axian was far more crowded on Ataghan's return trip. There were queues for food and tribute-charms, musicians who added to the crush by positioning themselves on every corner, and more younger women out and about with their friends. Ataghan strode on, knowing there would be time enough later for the semna-firi tents and keen to return to his compound.

Sehereden should be there by now resting under Ithreya's care but if Soaich had claimed the elddra, Fariye would need his comfort. He went straight to Sehereden's room but it was empty and he strode to the hall, expecting to see him propped in a seat, but only Mereya kept Ithreya company.

'Is Sehereden not back?' he demanded, fearing the party had come under attack.

'He's with Viv,' said Ithreya briefly. Ataghan grimaced but when he entered his room, he wondered if his lein kept vigil over a corpse. The fire was low and the lamps unlit, and there were long gaps between the elddra's labored breaths. Sehereden sat slumped to one side, and Fariye slept curled against her lein.

Ataghan carefully extricated Fariye and deposited her in her own bed, then came back, lit the lamps and hefted wood onto the fire. Sehereden said nothing, his hollow

160

eyes on the elddra. 'You should be resting,' said Ataghan finally.

'What did Baraghan say?'

'That if she still lives tomorrow, it will be by Enda's grace.'

'What of the arm?'

'Set and stitched.' Sehereden's gaze remained on the elddra and Ataghan softened his voice. 'Go to your bed, lein. I'll watch.'

'No.'

Sehereden rarely opposed him but he was in pain and raw from the elddra's deceit. 'I'll fetch some food,' said Ataghan, and went back to the hall. Ithreya had gone to her bed but Mereya loaded gorash, retsen, and a jug of semna on a tray and he took it back. They ate but Sehereden's attention remained on the elddra. Thankfully, there was no repeat of her ramblings.

'I met with the Genessi,' said Ataghan after a while. 'He seeks aid to destroy the Waradi sett that seeds the fighting.'

'And will you give it?' asked Sehereden, looking at him for the first time.

'That depends on our next meeting.'

'He used Viv as a messenger. What does he know of her?'

'He confirmed contact with her during your journey here, but wanted to *verify* my reputation before he approached. He helped her evade the traders after she freed the Lefer and asked her to deliver the message.'

'Nothing new to dispel the mystery that surrounds her,' muttered Sehereden. For a time, only the elddra's harsh breathing filled the room and as Sehereden's eyelids

161

drooped, Ataghan went to the window and thrust the shutters wide.

He wanted fresh air but as Fire Zadic lit the night sky and flooded the room with light, the sound of breathing ceased and Ataghan whirled. The elddra's eyes were open and fixed on its stars. 'Thris,' she whispered, her gaze so intense, Ataghan expected the mysterious Thris to appear behind him.

Sehereden roused and caught her hand. 'He'll come back for you, Viv, but you must stay here or he won't know where to find you. Stay with us Viv; stay with those who love you.' Sehereden's entreaty echoed Fariye's but her eyes closed, and her head lolled sideways.

He hastened back and searched for the pulse in her neck. It was slow and even, like the rise and fall of her chest. 'The fever's broken,' he said, and forced a smile for his lein. 'Enda's won.'

Chapter 22

Baraghan en-Esh-accom paused as Fire Zadic burst into the sky and a cheer went up from Axian's crowd. It marked the official start of the festivities but the air was already full of atunement's fine perfume and for all their puffed chests and swagger, Valen men were oblivious to it. Baraghan offered up ironic thanks to his forebears for a sense of smell so acute he knew when women were atuned often before they did, and that gave him a powerful advantage.

He could enjoy the semna-firi tents multiple times tonight *if* he chose, but since his visit to Ataghan en-Scinta-ril's compound, his thoughts had been elsewhere. Unusual for him, he conceded, as he sauntered across Axian, but understandable. He had last seen purple eyes and auburn curls in Astraal's halls, *rendered in paint*, and had never expected to see them in flesh and blood, least of all, in Esh-accom.

Ataghan en-Scinta-ril might deny her, as he denied so much else, but Baraghan had never wasted time wishing his mother had been less easily seduced. Astraali blood was a gift but like all gifts, extracted a price. He channeled its gnawing hunger better than the Scinta-ril's Syld, but still visited Soaich Square every Fire Zadic, in the hope the remoter vals had delivered more than battered Lefer.

His reconnoitre this zadic had revealed the usual array of tawdry wagons with their usual cargo but also a wagon he might have missed had he not just come from Ataghan's compound. Its canopy depicted a creature with black wings, which was unusual, but what had stopped him in his tracks was the creature's crudely painted crest of *curls*.

He picked his way across the slush, common sense telling him he was about to donate his traders to see another abused Lefer, handed over the entry price to the greasy-chinned wagoner, and made his way into the muddy enclosure. Heavy covers hid the wagon from those who had not paid, and smoke hid the wagon from those who had.

It came from a smouldering fire under the wagon and Baraghan positioned himself at the back of the enclosure where the air was cleaner. More spectators trickled in and, judging by their rustic clothing, from vals where Lefer and parien remained the exotic creatures of children's tales.

When the space could hold no more, Greasy-chin reappeared with a drum which, following a great deal of arm-flourishing, he began to beat. He gradually got faster, although not quickly enough for the audience, and as a mutter rose, he stopped and a blue-capped wagoner stepped forward. The *brains* of the operation, concluded Baraghan cynically.

'Good people of Esh-accom,' spruiked Blue-cap. 'Tonight, you are goin' to witness a truly amazin' sight. Tonight, you are goin' to see a sight no Valen has seen before. A sight that will be stayin' with you the length of your livin' days. For those of you who have seen a Lefer, do not be fearin' you'll be seein' the same again. Do not be worryin' another Lefer's to be revealed. For those of you who have heard of parien, who have *dreamed* of parien, maybe your dreams will be comin' true. Then again, maybe what you'll be seein' will surpass even those wondrous creatures.'

Greasy-chin gave the drum another thrashing and as the wagon's cover was pulled back, something was tossed on the fire to make the smoke blush red. Baraghan scarcely noticed. The cover revealed a man crouched in the cage's corner and the crowd hushed as they struggled to make sense of him. They would have seen the gold bird-like mask fixed to his face; the gold feathers glued to his skin; the briefest of gold loincloths that covered his genitals; and the strips of gold material that decorated his neck, upper arms, wrists, and ankles, but Baraghan saw his perfect musculature, his arms bound to his sides, and the effects of soporific herbs.

Nothing happened and a hiss started, as if the crowd believed they had been robbed, and Greasy-chin beat the drum again. 'Behold,' shouted Blue-cap, raising his arms in a flourish and Baraghan saw Greasy-chin tip something onto the fire.

There was a whoosh of acrid smoke that told Baraghan it was oil, and the crowd gasped as flames shot through the cage floor. For a moment, the smoke and flames obscured the man, and Baraghan feared he was to be incinerated but then he exploded from the pall, immense black wings thrashing, and cannoned into the top of the cage. He hung there, his wings smashing the bars as he fought to escape, and while the mask hid his face, his agony was plain.

The wagon's cover fell back into place, obscuring the spectacle, and white smoke billowed as the fire was extinguished. Someone in the crowd cheered, and others joined in, but many were silent, shocked by what they had seen. They shuffled out, Baraghan with them, and he was almost back to Axian before he trusted himself to stop. When he brought his knife down over the throats of

Blue-cap and Greasy-chin, there were not going to be any witnesses.

Viv's first awareness was of a burning thirst followed by smooth, warm, sheets against her skin. She was in a bed, naked, her injured arm bound to her side. The arm ached but with none of its former ferocity.

There was a jug of something nearby and mugs the same as in the arsehole's sett, so she guessed she was back there. She turned her head. Sehereden slept in a chair beside the bed, head back, his arm in a sling. She licked her chapped lips, looked at the jug again, and tried to sit but pain jagged and she swore. 'That was a *really* crap idea,' she muttered.

Sehereden's head jerked up. 'Viv,' he said hoarsely.

'Can you get me a drink? Water will be fine.'

He eased himself from the chair and filled a mug from the jug. 'Let me help you,' he said, and pushed pillows behind her back as she struggled to sit and simultaneously keep herself covered.

'We make a good pair,' he said as he handed her the mug. 'Only two functioning arms between us.' Viv drained the cold semna, and when he refilled the mug, drained it again. 'I'll get you some more,' he said, and went out.

Viv wondered who had undressed her but given Sehereden's injury, it had not been him. 'Is this your room?' she asked when he returned. The semna was warm this time and she drank it more slowly.

'Ataghan's. He brought you back from Esh-telin. He rides the fastest horse and you needed speed. Even if I hadn't been slashed, he'd have done it. I only got back yesterday evening and by then Baraghan had set your arm.

166

You came very close to death, Viv,' he added gently.

'Who's Baraghan?' asked Viv, ignoring his change of tone. Sehereden had made it clear what he thought of her at Esh-telin and she had no intention of churning over old ground.

'Baraghan is Esh-accom's best surgeon, in fact, he's probably the *Vale's* best surgeon. People don't survive a break like yours, Viv. It's called a Soaich break for good reason. Once the bone's through the skin, fever takes them. When Ataghan told me you had a Soaich break, I thought I'd lost you.'

'It takes a lot to kill an elddra,' said Viv flippantly.

'And a lot to make me understand what losing you meant. I told you on the journey here I was prepared to wait for your trust, but I wasn't as patient as I thought.' He half smiled. 'I've learned my lesson.'

Viv sighed. 'We've been through this before,' she said wearily. 'I haven't lied to you but what I haven't told you, what I *can't* tell you, probably amounts to the same thing. And I'm just passing through, remember? I know Valen men have lots of lovers, especially at Fire Zadic, but I've never wanted more than one. Forget about me, Sehereden. It's pretty clear Ithreya loves you, and she's Valen like you.'

Her throat tightened but it had nothing to do with deceit. She wanted this man with Rim's face but without his hard heart, and no matter how many times she told herself it was over, she had caved in and she would cave in again, unless … She licked her lips and took a steadying breath. 'There's something else Ithreya can give you, that I can *never* give you, and that's a child. I'm sterile, Sehereden.'

'Sterile?'

167

'Infertile, barren, whatever you call it here.' He looked at her blankly and she tried again. 'I've told you before how I've traded myself for food and shelter. I've been with lots of men, Sehereden, and I've never carried a child.'

'*Trading* yourself isn't the same as *gifting* yourself, Viv. A gift is given freely and there must be no coercion for Enda to grant a child. And the need for food and shelter is present in *every* zadic, whether Pool, Glimwing, or Horse, whereas children can only be seeded at Fire Zadic, when Enda grants atunement.'

Viv stared at him blankly. She had assumed Valen women were the same as those at home but they were not. They functioned more like cats and dogs and could only get pregnant when *atunement* kicked in, and *atunement* only kicked in at Fire Zadic. No wonder the air was thick with sexual tension. Atunement explained the tournaments, the festivities, and the tribute-charms. In fact, it explained *everything*.

And her being sterile was not the deal-breaker she envisaged. Sehereden believed that between his love, which would elicit her *gift*, and the star pattern sparkling in the sky, she would conceive, and she did not think repeating the doctor's lecture on hormones, or her lack of them, was going to change his mind.

'I'm not asking you for that gift now, Viv, not this Fire Zadic, I know you're not ready, but I am asking for forgiveness for Esh-telin.'

'Esh-telin wasn't your fault,' she said thickly, undone by his tenderness. She ran her fingers down the stubble of his jaw as she had before, and as before, it woke her physical need of him. Her hand curled under the silk of his hair and she pulled him close, their kiss long and deep, and then she rested her forehead against his.

She was aware of her nakedness, of his injury and her own, but the sense of him was like a balm that soothed the tension from her body. Her breathing fell into the same rhythm as his, and she closed her eyes. 'Sleep, Viv,' he said, and eased her back. His fingers lingered on her cheek, and she felt the brush of his lips, and then she let herself drift.

Chapter 23

Baraghan en-Esh-accom fought to order his thoughts as he strode through Esh-accom's streets. His preference was always for immediate action but what confronted him now was more complex than facing down the angry lein-trysts of women who had gifted themselves or side-stepping the arrogant demands of Esh-accom's Sylds.

At least one thing was clear: for all its grotesque baubles, the traders' creature was an Angellus, and Ataghan en-Scinta-ril's *guest* was as well. Their simultaneous appearance in The Wheel had to be more than a coincidence but why had the Angellus returned now, and why only two? It left them vulnerable, one already captive, the other safe only because of a powerful Syld's grudging care.

Baraghan fingered his knife as he considered last night's *entertainments*. The traders' knew better than to reveal what their captive really was, but not for the Angellus's sake. The Angellus were no more than Lefer to them: creatures to be or eaten, or traded, or exploited for coin. They had no understanding of the Angellus's majesty or the longing of those of Angellus blood to follow their forebears out of this world.

He needed to know more to ensure any plan of his succeeded and would start with the Angellus who remained free and undrugged, presuming she survived. He had no idea how she came to be lein of Ataghan en-Scinta-ril's daughter but it was clear Sehereden en-Scinta-ril sought her. It meant he would have to convince *his* lein of the Angellus's worth and Baraghan smiled sourly. While it was probably an impossible task, Sehereden had likely already carried out his own investigations, not that he would share his discoveries, and time was short.

Two elddra had lately arrived in Esh-accom which meant their masters might already know of the Angellus's return or soon would given last night's *amazin' spectacle*. As a *caring* surgeon, he had good reason to revisit Ataghan en-Scinta-ril's compound but not while the Syld was there and in the meantime, he had favours to call in.

Over the zadicans, he had stitched the flesh and set the bones of Stonash, Long-arms, traders, Sylds, Scharii, rustics from the remotest vals, and everyone in between. He charged no coin but his services were not free and some of those who owed him were about to clear their debts.

The second time Viv woke, she was clear-headed enough to consider how to quit the arsehole's bed without her clothes. She could wrap herself in a sheet, she supposed, like they did in movies, but it would be difficult with one arm bound to her side. Or she could dash naked across the passageway to Poss's room, but given her luck, Tormis would probably appear with a load of wood.

She had wedged herself up, no mean feat with one arm, when there was a knock at the door and Poss burst in, Ithreya behind her. 'Careful!' warned Ithreya, as Poss leapt onto the bed.

'Oh, you look so much better, lein,' said Poss, kneeling on the blankets to plant a kiss on Viv's cheek. 'Da said you were going to die, but I said you weren't, and Baraghan fixed your arm, he's the best healer in Esh-accom, but you had fever, and your breathing was awful, but I told you how much I loved you, and that you had to stay, and you did!' Poss drew breath. 'Does your arm still hurt, lein?'

171

'Not as much, Poss.'

'Ser said his doesn't hurt as much either, but he won't be able to compete in the tournaments. Da said you both got hurt in some fighting. Fara got hurt too. Ser's upset that Fara's not here but da said he'll bring Fara back when he's not lame anymore.'

Ithreya would have found it hard to get a word in even had she tried, but she waited, her face a mask. 'Brithergen's here with da,' rattled on Poss, 'and da says I can go to Brithergen's compound today *if* I like. I've got friends there now like Sithi and Rael and Morva, but I wanted to see you first.'

'Brithergen's compound sounds like fun,' said Viv.

'It is! I'll see you tomorrow, lein, or maybe the next day.' She gave Viv another kiss and then her footsteps echoed back up the passageway.

'I'm also pleased to see you're recovering,' said Ithreya politely.

'I just need some clothes so I can give the Syld back his room,' said Viv, horribly aware of Ithreya's coldness.

'I'll fetch some for you,' said Ithreya.

Viv contemplated all Ithreya had done for her while she waited and how Viv had *thanked* her by taking the man Ithreya loved. It sounded like some bloody Soap Opera, but it was pretty accurate. Ithreya returned and silently helped Viv into the clothes, even carefully unbinding her arm and fashioning a sling while Viv racked her brains for something to say.

'Sehereden said you came off Fara at Esh-telin,' said Ithreya, as she buttoned Viv's jacket. He said you knew it would come under Waradi attack because you claimed to have been there earlier that day.'

172

Viv knew she should let it go, but the word *claimed* grated. 'I *was* there earlier that day.'

Ithreya paused, as if to give Viv time to tell the truth, then half shrugged. 'I've never considered Sehereden en-Scinta-ril a fool, but he seems to be where you're concerned. His lein, however, isn't a fool. Come Glimwing, I hope Sehereden sees with greater clarity too *and* makes *better* choices.' Ithreya's colour was high which told Viv just how upset she was. 'Sehereden is sleeping now and I ask that you let him be, so his healing can begin.'

'Of course,' said Viv, taken aback by the inference she would go and demand sex. Ithreya nodded curtly and the door snapped shut behind her. *Well, that went well, Vivi. Guess ya lucky ya ain't wearin' scratch marks down ya face.* 'It's a crap-heap, Rim,' she muttered.

She had no idea whether Ithreya had gone to her room or to the hall where the arsehole and Brithergen probably still were, and made her way gingerly down the passageway and out of the compound. The gentle light suggested late afternoon and the air was sweet with the scent of flowers, but Viv went slowly, her legs unsteady.

The sound of the festivities grew as she neared Axian and she turned down a quiet side street. It was lined with compounds too but the warped timbers of the wooden walls revealed the poorer buildings beyond. Viv expected the street to be crossed by others but it was not and she trudged on, hoping for a seat where she could rest. Esh-accom did not seem to have any of the civic groups who usually provided such things, she concluded dryly, as she leaned against a wall to catch her breath. It had been a mistake not to eat before setting out especially if she had been as close to death as Sehereden and Poss claimed.

173

She turned at the sound of footsteps. Just children, she concluded, but there was something chillingly familiar about the small, cloaked figures. Her arm was in a sling under her shirt and jacket, neither of which she could unbutton quickly with one hand, and she was in no shape to run. Her heart thudded as the Stonash's hooded-eyes slid sideways but they kept on going and Viv breathed again. They had no reason to dislike her, she reasoned, even if, by some odd chance, it was their caravan that had dragged her into the ice fire.

She struggled on, increasingly light-headed, and was relieved to see another street ahead but then a man rounded the corner, saw her and he quickened his pace. 'This bloody day just keeps on getting better,' she muttered, and then her knees buckled, and the man was suddenly beside her.

'It is too early for you to be from your bed, Violet Iris Vacia, even if you are Angellus,' he said, swept her into his arms, and carried her away.

Baraghan had been well pleased with his day's work even before the female Angellus had stumbled into his keeping and he could thank Ataghan en-Scinta-ril for adding to the day's achievements, yet it was anger that simmered as he strode along. Ataghan's hatred would destroy him in the end, as it destroyed others of his kind, but Baraghan was determined it would not destroy Violet Iris Vacia.

She was as light as he expected and her scent stronger now she no longer hovered near death. He inhaled deeply and his yearning was so intense he momentarily forgot his whereabouts, then awareness returned making him conscious of her tension. 'Forgive me, Violet Iris Vacia,' he said, 'for having failed to introduce myself. I am Baraghan en-Esh-accom, the surgeon who set and stitched your arm. You've been unwise to test your strength so early but I blame the hospitality of your host, or more likely, his *lack* of hospitality.'

'I'm feeling better now. You can put me down.'

'You don't and I won't. Friends have a compound nearby where you can recover properly before I *regretfully* return you to Ataghan en-Scinta-ril's *care*.'

The compound turned out to be as shabby as the others she had passed and Baraghan bawled commands as he strode across the yard into the building. A fair-haired woman appeared, along with several older men, and a boy with a thick mop of reddish-brown hair, and Baraghan flung still more orders as he continued down the passageway.

Viv doubted they were *friends*, given the way Baraghan threw his weight about, but they did not seem to be servants either. He kicked open a door and carried her into a room made snug by a fire, deposited her gently on a couch, then laid his hand against her forehead. His eyes were dark blue up close, but he did not look at her even when he shifted his hand to the pulse in her neck, just gazed into the middle distance.

'Too warm, and too erratic,' he muttered and pulled her face close to his. Viv jerked back and gasped as pain tore through her arm. 'I must beg forgiveness a second time,' he said. 'I learned a great deal about you today but not, it seems, all things. I intend only to deliver you my breath.' Viv stared at him blankly. 'An elddric's breath aids healing *if* permitted.'

Viv nodded, desperate to ease the pain in her arm and he leaned in again and matched his breathing to hers. The pain dulled and her thoughts swung to how Thris's sweet breath had eased her pain, and anger, and sorrow.

Baraghan called himself elddric and her *Angellus*, and while his interest in her healing seemed genuine, she sensed he had other motivations. There was a knock and the fair-haired woman and the boy appeared with tocki, mugs, and a jug. Baraghan thanked them with more courtesy than he had shown earlier and poured Viv a drink. She expected it to be semna but it was a lot sweeter.

'My special recipe,' he said, noting her expression. 'You must eat too. Angellus exist in exquisite balance *until* they're injured.'

'Is the boy your son?' she asked, ignoring his second allusion to Angellus.

'It's a woman's prerogative to name her child's father,' said Baraghan, as he relaxed back on the couch, 'especially when she's lein-trysted. But yes, he's my son.'

'Doesn't her lein-tryst mind?'

'The boy's *seed-father*? Why should he mind?' Baraghan's arrogance reminded her of Kald's, and she wondered how many women Baraghan had *charmed* into deceiving their lein-trysts. 'You don't approve, Violet Iris Vacia?'

'I don't like deceit.'

'And yet you practice it every day,' said Baraghan with a smile. 'You let the Valen call you elddra and endure their contempt because their spiteful disdain is the least of your problems.' He refilled her mug. 'I don't condemn you for it, Violet Iris Vacia. I face some of the same difficulties myself.'

'My name's Viv.'

'A name too small for the wondrous beauty of an Angellus.'

'I'm not Angellus.'

'The Angellus who once made their home in The Wheel were male. You're the female of their kind, whatever you name yourself.' He smiled again. 'I wait to see whether your ability to deceive is limited to *allowing* others to continue their malicious and ignorant beliefs, as the Angellus's was, or whether you can *actually* lie.' His dark blue eyes bored into hers and Viv swallowed dryly. 'I thought so,' he murmured. 'If it's any consolation, I can't lie either and strangely enough, it might aid us in what lies ahead.'

Chapter 24

Viv contemplated him as he placed another tocki on her plate. She got the impression from Sehereden that the elddric were an even more shameful product of *mixed-marriages* than elddra but Baraghan was completely at ease.

'You'll need to eat at least three more tocki before we go,' he said, 'and drink another couple of mugs of semna. Your weakness makes you even more vulnerable. I've spent the day gathering information about you, amongst other things, and know you've met with the elddra here and that Sehereden en-Scinta-ril, the man who desires you as lein-tryst, has too, presumably to discover your history.

'And I imagine that the elddra he and you met with painted their masters, the Daimon, with a nobler brush than the Astraali, but they're both the same.' He shrugged. 'Oh, the Astraali enjoy their petty powers more than the Daimon, but all who carry the Angellus's blood yearn to dwell with their forebears.

'And so, one way or another, The Wheel is full of spies, Violet Iris Vacia. The Scharii, the elddra, the Stonash with their urrut caravans trekking back and forth to Ourassin; the tournaments and festivals with their wagoners from distant vals; it doesn't take very long for news of *unusual things* to spread but understanding what *unusual things* portend, is another matter entirely.

'Simple folk see with simple eyes, and their claims are easily dismissed, while others are blinded by hatred. Elddra are red-haired, blue-eyed, heal quickly and are secretive hence, you are elddra. But elddra don't take children as leins, search for their mothers, risk themselves for Lefer, survive a Soaich break, or care that Valen murder each other's families.

'Nor do they have purple depths to their eyes, lustrous hair, or the fineness of form the elddra's diluted blood robbed them of zadicans ago. And while the elddra hold Valen in contempt, they're not ignorant of Valen ways *as you are*.'

'What is it you want?' asked Viv, more steadily than she felt.

'Obviously, I want you to open the door you came through, so I can leave by it. However, given the nature of the Angellus's arrival *and* departure, I presume you're bound by certain prohibitions. If I were an elddric whose Angellus blood expressed itself in violence, I would threaten you with pain and injury, but I'm not. Instead, I propose a trade. You have something I greatly desire, and I have something you greatly desire.'

Viv's heart gave an uncomfortable thud. 'You've found my mother?'

'I've found Thrisdane.'

Ataghan made his way through Axian's evening crowds more at ease than he had been for many days. He had enjoyed the practice bouts at Brithergen and Drasen's compounds despite their men having tested him far less than Sehereden. The closeness of leins meant they anticipated each other's moves but Sehereden's injury had put an end to their practice sessions.

Brithergen's bustling compound had also reminded him that his own sett had once been filled with the dash of children in games of Chase and Hide, the slower movements of the old, and the quieter grace of women, and he grimly considered his second meeting with Quen en-Sar-ril.

The man was no fool and even if obliterating the lair at the Perin-ril failed to stop the Waradi's poisonous invasions, it would remind them there was a price to pay for their murdering. He and Quen had agreed on a time and place for the attack, but it would have to wait until after Fire Zadic. The Waradi, like other Valen, journeyed to bigger settlements to celebrate the festivities and the Perin-ril would be deserted.

Ataghan had started the day early at Axian's rinks, not because he had any interest in those who fought, given they must win many rounds to earn the right to face him, but to remind the spectators of his status. Then he had gone to the semna-firi tents where he had not waited long before he had gifted his tribute-charms and in turn, been gifted the chance to father.

The day would have ended well had Ithreya not sent a message to report the elddra's disappearance *and* to blame herself for it. Ataghan's mouth hardened. Men and women rarely fought over each other *unless* lein-trysts were involved, which was yet another reason to avoid them. It was usual for men to seek the favours of *many* women during Fire Zadic to increase their chances of being gifted a child and for women to gift themselves to *many* men to increase their chances of carrying, but from the moment Ithreya had ridden into Esh-accom, it was clear she wanted Sehereden as a lein-tryst.

Ithreya was beautiful by any measure with the blue eyes Sehereden favoured and would have been assured of a lein-tryst had the party not included the elddra, and despite the elddra's duplicity at Esh-telin, Sehereden's commitment to her had grown. Ataghan's brows drew.

No doubt she had spent the day making more mischief and he turned his feet towards Soaich Square. Given her injuries the elddra should have spent the day resting at his compound, but she might well have gone back to Soaich Square just to spite him.

Coloured lamps lit the way but there was no disguising the mud and his mood worsened as it caked his boots and then, sure enough, he saw her in the crowd ahead. At least she had the wits to covered her hair but her companion had not bothered and Baraghan's red-brown mane had always made him conspicuous.

Ataghan's hand strayed to his knife as he picked his way over forward. Given Baraghan's predilections, it was no surprise he had reacquainted himself with the *beauty*, but why bring her here? She had already demonstrated her hatred of the Lefer's confinement and it was a hatred Baraghan shared.

Ataghan's breath hissed. Baraghan planned something and Ataghan sensed it was not going to end well. He held the elddra as they walked, not as a lover might, but to support her, and Ataghan's eyes narrowed as they stopped at a wagon. Its canopy was adorned with the usual crude depiction of its wares but the spruiker was nearing the end of his spiel to view *a truly life-changin' event* and as people hurried forward Ataghan stepped sideways to scrape the mud from his boots and let the men behind him pass.

He recognised the blonde head of Ithreya's brother Galian among the group who now obscured him should Baraghan glance back. Baraghan had reached the top of the queue and was busy handing over his traders and then Ataghan saw him smooth his hair.

The finger flick would have passed unnoticed by those who had never fought but Ataghan scanned swiftly. Long-arms disappeared beyond the wagon, three men loitered to his right, and another joined his *friends* in the queue in front. There were Stonash there too, hoods drawn low.

Ataghan paid his traders and positioned himself to the side, close to the exit. Lamps threw a light made murky by smoke, but he could see Baraghan and the elddra towards the front of the wagon. Baraghan was tense but the elddra looked like she had turned to stone.

The spruiker was replaced by a thumping drum and the smoke turned red as the canopy was heaved up. Ataghan did not see what the cage held, the elddra's face so full of horror, he found it hard to drag his eyes away. Baraghan said something to her and when she made no response, repeated it more forcefully and she nodded, but her eyes stayed on the cage and Ataghan snatched a glance that way in time to see an explosion of fire.

A winged-creature flew from the flames and smashed into the top of the cage as it fought to escape and then there was a scream so terrible that people looked away from the spectacle to search for its source. It was not his daughter's lein, thank Enda, but it *was* an elddra. She broke from the crowd and threw herself shrieking at the cage.

There were more shouts as people pointed at the cage's roof. Stonash clambered over it and their kin, the Long-arms, swung along its sides. Ataghan was shoved sideways as a wagoner rushed forward, only to be stopped by a fist, and fights broke out between the wagoners intent on helping their comrades, and those determined to stop them.

Billowing black smoke added to the confusion and Ataghan realised someone should have doused the flames, as did the crowd, who surged towards the exit. The Long-arms swung clear as flames licked the canopy, and Ataghan thought they had abandoned the creature to its fate, but then it burst from the cage and he lost sight of it.

He had no time to search the night skies; knives flashed which told him the fight had turned deadly and he fought his way to where Baraghan and the elddra had been. Baraghan was on the ground, fending off a wagoner's knife thrusts, and men brawled to either side but the elddra remained motionless, oblivious to her danger.

Ataghan snatched her up and as Galian appeared, thrust her into his arms. 'Take her to my compound,' he ordered, then slammed his heel into the wagoner's ankle. The man screamed and Ataghan's boot smashed his wrist next, sending the knife spinning into the mud. Then he wrenched Baraghan to his feet. 'Go,' he shouted, and they ran.

Thris streaked through the night sky, a blind thing, bound, and burned. His wings thrashed with the fire-triggered ferocity of the cage, but the cage was gone and he rocketed on, faster and faster. Citrus streamed from his skin and his heart thundered, but he was deaf to what it threatened. The forests gave way to plains, then to a waterfall's fume, then to shining mountains that ringed a perfect lake. Blood flooded his eyes and his heart faltered and stopped. He fell from the sky and in the Blue Helixai, Ash woke from his slumbers and screamed.

Ataghan led as they ran, taking the back streets, knives at the ready, and they did not speak until they reached Baraghan's compound. No one followed but the wagoners had their own networks of eyes and ears, and word would spread. Baraghan took a jug of semna to his room and Ataghan drained his first mug in a single gulp. 'What in Soaich's name possessed you to take the elddra to the entertainments?' he panted.

'I didn't take her, she was a happy surprise, and a useful one at that.'

'Not *that* elddra! My daughter's lein!'

'You mean the Angellus. I needed to demonstrate the truth of my claim.' Baraghan unstopped a bottle of strong smelling liquid and dabbed the cuts on his hands.

Ataghan rounded on him. 'What claim?'

'That the wagoners held her fellow Angellus.'

'A Lefer plastered with feathers and gold paint,' spat Ataghan, pouring himself a second mug and prowling around the room.

Baraghan paused in mid dab. 'I've thought you many things over the zadicans, Ataghan, but never a fool. You saw the Angellus's reaction? Unsurprising given what she witnessed.'

'It was hard to witness *anything* in that smoke!'

'The wagoners should have quenched the flames,' admitted Baraghan, 'but it ended well.'

Ataghan slammed his mug down. 'If you think this has ended then *you're* the fool.'

'It's ended for me, well almost. Remind the Angellus of our agreement, will you *once* she's recovered. And take good care of her, Ataghan. It's hard to see someone you love all but burned to death.'

Chapter 25

Ataghan considered Baraghan's claims as he strode back to his compound. He took the less used streets, knives at the ready. It would be easy to dismiss Baraghan as a man long on passion and short on judgement but wrong. Baraghan yearned for the mythical gateway the Angellus had supposedly left by, but *if* it existed, Ataghan hoped it would never be discovered. A gate used to exit, could be used to enter, and the Angellus were testament to the damage *that* caused.

Ataghan wondered what deal the elddra had struck with Baraghan to liberate the creature. Baraghan did nothing for free; those who fought the wagoners tonight had done so to discharge their debts. There had been plenty of witnesses too, eager to ingratiate themselves with Esh-accom's Sylds.

At least his daughter's lein had not been involved, and those who had been had already slipped back into anonymity. The Valen found it hard to differentiate between individual Stonash and Long-arms anyway, so the only Valen clearly identifiable were him and Baraghan.

Ataghan swore. The Sylds had already reprimanded him over his elddra's behaviour but it was the *older* elddra who had been central to the disturbance and he abruptly found himself in agreement with Baraghan that her presence there had been fortuitous.

It would be wise if Baraghan did leave for a time, as he had hinted, but what of himself? His main contribution had been to remove one of the key combatants, something he had done before, but if the Sylds really wanted to take him to task, he would quit Esh-accom too, and take their wager-tributes with him.

Ithreya was in the hall with Galian when he returned and leapt up. 'Syld, Viv is—' but Ataghan turned to her choose-brother.

'I'm indebted to you for your aid, Galian. It was a happy chance you were at the *entertainments* tonight.' He poured himself some semna and settled opposite. Ithreya was agitated, but he kept his attention on her choose-brother. 'Of course, the *entertainments* aren't usually so . . . *entertaining*.'

'So my choose-sister tells me. It's my first visit to Esh-accom and I was keen to see what was on offer.'

'Many more enjoyable things than captive Lefer,' said Ataghan as he topped up Galian's mug.

'It didn't look like a Lefer,' said Galian doubtfully.

'You've been to the Leferen?'

'No …'

'They're very different in their natural state. By the time they've been jolted about in wagons for days on end, beaten, starved, and daubed with noxious paints and glues, they could be anything.'

'Syld, Viv is *very* unwell,' broke in Ithreya.

'Unsurprising, given she joined the rough and tumble of the festivities so soon after a Soaich break.'

'It's not her arm. I think I should wake Sehereden.'

'You'll let him sleep,' said Ataghan sharply, then smiled at Galian as he rose. 'Please excuse me while I check on my guest.'

186

Fariye's room was stifling, thanks to the blazing fire, and both lamps had been lit, but all he could see in the bed was the top of the elddra's head. She had curled into a ball, face tucked down, legs drawn up hard against her chest. Her good arm clutched her head and her breathing was as harsh as when she had been fevered.

He lifted the cover from her face but she continued to stare straight ahead as she had at the entertainments. 'Elddra?' Nothing; he took a turn around the room. *It's hard to see someone you love all but burned to death.*

Baraghan believed the creature was the elusive Thrisdane *and* Angellus, but what Ataghan had gleaned about Thrisdane suggested he was Valen. The elddra's panting set Ataghan on edge and he strode to the window, angry at being confined with her again. Younger band members panted like that after their first battle but not for this long.

Why in Enda's name had she gone to the entertainments anyway? She must have known what she would see *unless* Baraghan had convinced her she would see her longed for lover. There had been a lot of smoke, and the older elddra's screams had added to the confusion, but if the elddra *did* believe her lover had returned, her interest in Sehereden would wane and something good might have come out of the night after all.

Her rasping continued and he reluctantly leaned over and breathed into her mouth, paused, and repeated the process. It made no difference and he had just decided to leave the elddra to sleep it off when Sehereden burst in. He went straight to the bed, pulled the elddra onto his lap, and flipped the cover over them both. 'Ithreya told me what happened,' he said, his attention fixed on her. 'Was it Thrisdane?'

187

'It was hard to tell what the creature was.'

'It must have been him. She wouldn't be like this otherwise.'

Sehereden murmured reassurances as he held her close and Ataghan rose. 'Don't over tire yourself, lein,' he said, but as he pulled the door closed behind him, he doubted Sehereden had even heard him.

Viv was locked in a never-ending nightmare of women being dragged to the pyre, only to transform into Thris with his bound hands and empty eyes. Sometimes as the flames took hold, his wings became fiery brands and other times, charred stumps, and always when she looked into his eyes, darkness looked back. She was lost to him, as he was lost to her, in a world of endless burning. Breathing was hard, as if she breathed smoke, and her joints stiff, as if she were bound, and the horror was so great that in the dream, she wished only for death.

And then, amongst the flames, a quietness grew, like the quiet that centres a maelstrom, then expanded, pushing the flames before it, to leave an emptiness that scent could enter, and human warmth, and words she could not return. She was held mute by a grief that threatened to tear her apart but in the end, even that grief gave way to exhaustion, and exhaustion to awareness.

She knew Sehereden's voice, the beat of his heart strong against her cheek, the arms that held her close and the terror of the night at bay, and with that knowing came a hunger for comfort and she dragged her eyes open. 'You're here,' she said in wonder and touched the soft stubble of his jaw. His was a human face, with human failings and human understandings. 'I want you,' she said hoarsely.

'Viv, this isn't a good time.'

'Because you're in pain?'

'We're *both* in pain but I didn't mean that. You're very distressed. I don't know what happened at the festivities, but …'

'Don't!' she said, putting her fingers to his lips. 'I want you.'

'Here? Now?' he asked, needing to be sure.

'Yes. Here and now.'

Viv had no idea how they made love in the Vale and she no longer cared. She struggled out of her shirt and the sling, then helped Sehereden out of his shirt, careful to avoid his bandaged shoulder but could not recall later how the rest of their clothes came off, just the delicious feel of his skin next to hers.

Their brief encounter in the maark had woken her hunger for him and she slid herself on top and kissed him deeply to inhale his male scent. His finger-tips traced sensuous trails down the curve of her shoulder and dip of her back, and his lips moved from her neck to her breasts to her mouth in an exquisite cycle.

She was desperate for his comfort but he slowed her, submerging her in a swirling sea of pleasure. Rim's love-making had sometimes been brutal and always self-serving and joining angelically with Thris had delivered an ecstasy as wondrous as the stars, but far more fleeting. Now Sehereden took her to the brink and eased her back again as he subtly tested what heightened her desire. Viv wondered whether it was how all Valen men made love to secure their precious children or whether it was just

Sehereden and then she wondered nothing at all, as he brought them both to climax.

She lay in his arms afterwards, enveloped in a delicious languor and after a time, propped on her elbow to look at him. The lamps had guttered but the glow of fire-ashes was enough to light the lines about his mouth that told of pain. 'I've hurt your shoulder,' she said.

'No. You've healed me.' He smiled and smoothed the curls from her eyes.

'I need a hair-cut.'

'Why not grow it and braid it as Valen women do?' he said, as he ran his fingers through her curls.

'Because I'm not a Valen woman.'

Viv regretted the words the moment they left her mouth. They reminded them both of all the things left unsaid, but Sehereden's caress did not falter. 'No, you're not, are you? You're Violet Iris Vacia, better known as Viv.' His voice was lightly teasing, but his face was serious. 'And lovelier than I could ever have imagined possible.'

'Not disappointed then?' asked Viv, made self-conscious by his intensity.

His hand stilled. 'How could I be disappointed?'

Viv shrugged and looked away, but his hand turned her face back to his. 'Never doubt how deserving you are of love, Viv, and how loving you are. And never doubt my feelings for you that are not just for now, *for Fire Zadic*, but for all the zadicans to come.'

'That's a long time, Sehereden,' she said with a poor attempt at a smile. 'My life so far has taught me *not* to make predictions.'

'Maybe your life *so far* needs to end, and a new life begin.'

'I've made a deal with Baraghan,' she said abruptly.

'A *deal*?'

'A trade in return for what he did last night. It means I have to leave Esh-accom for a while.'

Sehereden's brows drew. 'What sort of trade?'

'I can't tell you, but it's not me. I'm not trading myself.'

'Was it Thrisdane he released from the cage?' Viv took a shaky breath. She still found it hard to even think about last night and knowing Thris was a long way from safe made it worse. 'Was it, Viv?' prompted Sehereden but she still could not speak. 'Ataghan said it was hard to see what the creature was, but Ithreya's choose-brother described it as a winged-man.' Sehereden's fingers caressed her cheek. 'What is he, Viv?'

'Do leins have secrets, Sehereden?'

He blinked. 'What …'

'Do they?'

'Leins are one as I've said.'

'So, your lein will know you've spent the night with me?'

'He won't ask. It's a woman's right to reveal who she's gifted herself to, *if* she chooses, not the man's. And you haven't answered my question.'

'You'll pass on anything I say to the arsehole, won't you?'

Sehereden grimaced. 'You need to build trust with him, Viv.'

'His hatred of me won't change and believe me, it's mutual.'

'Is Thrisdane Angellus?' he asked directly.

'I've heard the Angellus disappeared long ago.'

'That's not an answer.'

'No, it isn't, is it?'

Sehereden extricated himself from the bed and Viv watched him dress. She had ruined their intimacy but the sight of Sehereden's muscled neck and shoulders provided *some* compensation. 'This is why I don't make predictions,' she said, as he reached for the door.

He turned back, his face gentle again. 'Rest, Viv. You need time to heal.'

Chapter 26

Viv struggled to dress herself with one hand and only hunger and thirst drove her on. She wore the sling over top her jacket this time and hoped she would soon be able to discard it altogether. She had no idea how late it was, having taken Sehereden's advice to rest and fallen sleep. Thankfully, it had been a sleep empty of dreams and all she needed now was Mereya's semna and stew to get her back on an even keel.

Mereya was not in the hall but Ithreya was and jumped up when Viv appeared. 'I'm so glad you've recovered,' she said in relief.

'I'm feeling better, thank you,' said Viv uncomfortably. It was easier to deal with Ithreya's dislike, than her kindness, especially after all the *gifting* that had gone on last night.

'Sit, and I'll get you some food. Sehereden said you'd need to eat and drink, and Mereya made a special batch of gorash.' Viv wondered whether Sehereden had gone straight from her bed to Ithreya's, then reminded herself that *she* had initiated the sex and if anyone had a right to be jealous, it was Ithreya.

'We can resume our tour of Esh-accom later, if you feel well enough,' said Ithreya, as Viv ate. 'It's far pleasanter now Vorash's finished. The Syld will compete in his first tournament tonight too. It's more an exhibition bout than anything else because Esh-accom's Sylds like their champions to give Esh-accom's visitors a taste of what's to come.'

To encourage more betting, presumed Viv, and increase the Sylds' slice of the pie. She did not want to see the arsehole compete but nor did she want to be stuck in the compound. Mecenth had not known of any women in Esh-accom who looked like Viv but being out and about increased Viv's chances of seeing her mother *if* she had visited.

Ithreya had implied a tour of all of Esh-accom but she seemed reluctant to go beyond Axian's glittering stalls. Beautifully crafted copper and silverware, gem-set wooden bowls, and swatches of metal-threaded cloth vied for attention, while food stalls filled the air with the spicy smell of cooking and musicians plied their trade to add to the holiday atmosphere.

Ithreya looped her arm through Viv's and Viv started to relax as they strolled between the stalls. It was a perfect evening, like those at home after a long hot day, and coloured lanterns were hoisted aloft as the first dull stars glimmered.

Ithreya stopped at a stall that traded children's jewellery and flicked through a rack of enameled bracelets. 'Which do you think Fariye would like?' she asked, holding up a red and a turquoise one.

'She seems to like anything pretty,' said Viv, appreciating Ithreya's effort to include her in the decision.

'Turquoise would suit her, I think. She's inherited her mother's fair skin though not her blue eyes.'

Viv blinked in surprise. 'You've met her mother?'

'Once, when I was young. Sirenya of the auburn hair,' she added with a smile. 'Sirenya was distant kin to me and stayed at our compound after Fariye's birth. Then she went to Astraal and was only there a short while before she died. My father said those of Astraal care little for each other.' Viv wondered if Sirenya's death was behind the arsehole's hatred of all things Astraali.

'So, she made the Syld choose-father before she went,' she muttered, struggling to understand how Sirenya could walked away from her newborn daughter.

'It was rumoured she wanted a lein-tryst and left when the Syld refused it,' said Ithreya softly. 'He was only twenty then and already winning tournaments. He probably thought he would be offered many choose-children over the zadicans.'

But he had not, realised Viv and cynically wondered whether his lovers were reluctant to leave their children with so violent a man. Then again, she had seen him be nothing but loving with Fariye, and Fariye certainly loved him.

A bell sounded above the hubbub, and Ithreya hurriedly completed the trade. 'The tournaments are about to start,' she said and set off through the crowd, taking Viv with her. The spectators were already several rows deep but she saw Galian's blonde head and Drasen's darker one beside him, and they created a space for she and Ithreya to wedge in beside them.

A man in a gold-trimmed sash held court in the centre of the rink as he extolled the virtues of the previous champions' *exemplary skills* and the whole performance went on for some time given the arsehole's *exemplary skills* were extensive, but his spruiking reminded Viv of the *entertainments* and she took a steadying breath.

She had never liked crowds and pulled her injured arm close to her body as people pressed in around them. There was no sign of the arsehole or Sehereden, but there were gaudy tents at the back of the rink where she guessed they waited. The arsehole's competitor was afforded no such luxury but waited in the rink, glaring at the crowd from under lowered brows like a street-fighter.

The arsehole finally appeared, *with* Sehereden, and stepped into the rink. He looked a lot calmer than his adversary but Rim had looked laid-back too. The arsehole did not look at the other man, or at the crowd, just stared straight ahead in a manner that reminded Viv of harmonising.

His stillness added to his sense of menace and the crowd hushed, then the spruiker exited the rink and the bell rang. The street-fighter sprinted forward, quicker than the arsehole, so that they clashed near the arsehole's corner, not that it made any difference. The man was on his back in the sand so quickly Viv missed how it happened.

The arsehole's second adversary was taller, with a longer reach than the arsehole's, but the result was the same, and Viv stared at the arsehole in morbid fascination. His razor-sharp reflexes were like Rim's but his grace reminded her of Thris. The arsehole shared *nothing* with Thris, she asserted acidly, and searched for an escape route but those packed in around her were in no mood to shift.

The third competitor was of similar build to the arsehole and Viv wondered if he would present more of a challenge. Perhaps he did, given the bout lasted five seconds, not two, the extra time taken by the arsehole's feint, which left the man spread-eagled.

The arsehole quit the rink and there was great deal of cheering and applause. 'He's going to be hard to beat,' said Drasen as they moved away.

'Has he *ever* been beaten?' asked Galian excitedly.

'Mecenth remembers him being beaten seven or eight zadicans ago,' said Ithreya, 'but he always makes the final rounds and Esh-accom's Syld's can thank him for the healthy state their coffers.'

'He gets a cut too,' said Drasen, 'though I don't think it's the reason he competes. Amethen says his urrut herds are pretty healthy.'

'Sehereden believes he'll win this zadican too,' said Ithreya.

'He's hardly likely to say his lein will lose,' pointed out Drasen.

'Sehereden believes he'll win because of the Waradi and Ascadi,' continued Ithreya. 'He says you only lose those fights once.'

'I suppose it *would* hone your skills,' said Galian but Drasen sobered and Viv guessed he had experienced more bloodshed than Ithreya's choose-brother. He took Ithreya's arm but Viv cradled her injured arm with her good one to stop Galian becoming more *familiar*.

'I'm pleased to see you're recovered, Viv,' he said, as they followed Ithreya and Drasen through the crowds. 'The Syld charged me with returning you to his compound last night, which I was happy to do. I find cruelty to wild creatures upsetting,' he added.

'Thank you,' said Viv, hoping the word covered everything she should be grateful for *without* encouraging him. Ithreya and Drasen had stopped at a stall and Viv feigned interest in its offerings while she considered how to extricate herself from Galian's company.

'The stars are pretty, or do you prefer the birds?' asked Galian.

'What?' He held up several tribute-charms and Viv blinked as she took in the stall's wares. Drasen had already added one to those Ithreya wore and Viv's gaze jerked back to Galian. 'They're all lovely Galian but elddra don't

197

wear them,' she said, as graciously as she could. Luckily Sehereden's chain and charm were safely in her pocket with the tryst-bracelet.

Galian dipped his head but she knew she had offended him, and she nodded awkwardly and making an exaggerated show of protecting her injured arm, slipped through a gap in the crush and kept going until she reached a less crowded part of Axian.

There was a line of brocaded tents to her left with ornate tables and chairs set under the canopy at the front. Coloured glass decanters and glasses sat on gold trays, and she noticed a couple finish their drinks and slip behind the curtain at the back. Well, the Valen might have their flaws but being prudes certainly was not one of them!

There was no sign of Galian, which was a relief, and Viv was considering how to spend the rest of the evening when the arsehole and Sehereden emerged from the crowd. An entourage of young men and women trailed in their wake and the whole group headed for the sex-tents. Sehereden would have seen her, had he glanced her way, but he was intent on the beautiful black-haired woman on his arm.

Viv turned in the opposite direction, struggling to keep her face empty of her feelings. No doubt he would soon be telling the woman how much he wanted her trust, and how patiently he would wait for it! None of the men here made any secret of seeking *gifts*, she reminded herself, and it was a two-way flow, given she had just seen Ithreya accept a tribute-charm from Drasen, but knowing did nothing to quell her anger.

Get a grip, Vivi. Ya just crap at judging men. Ya chose the angel man who loves the starry lands of the Great Beyond, then the handsome man who loves his lein. Preceded by you, Rim, who only loves himself, she retorted.

Couples strolled by hand in hand, just to reinforce how alone she was, and she searched for somewhere quiet and noticed she was near the Old Quarter. Its tall trees would be a pleasant place to kill some time but as she considered paying them a return visit, an elddra emerged from one of its streets.

Chapter 27

At first Viv thought it was the elddra Drasen had mentioned but it was Anetherey. She was disheveled, as if she had run, and Viv recalled she had been at the *entertainments* last night. Anetherey stopped at the building-line and gazed about wildly. Her eyes passed over Viv then jerked back, and she hastened forwards with such single-minded intensity Viv was tempted to dissolve back into the crowd. And she might have, had she not believed Anetherey would give chase.

Anetherey's hair had come loose from its neat braid and swirled around her face in disarray. 'Where is he, *Violetirisvacia*?' she demanded, so close that Viv stepped back.

'I don't know.'

'You must know! You're of his kind. Tell me!'

Anetherey was on the edge of violence and the last thing Viv wanted was a disturbance to give Esh-accom's Sylds another excuse to flex their pompous muscles. 'This isn't a good place to speak of such things,' she said softly, as if the passing lovers were spies. 'We need somewhere quieter.' Anetherey's eyes jerked around the scattered crowd. 'The Old Quarter,' whispered Viv, hoping to God Anfarena searched for her missing companion.

She set off down the street she had used last time, Anetherey at her shoulder. The elddra muttered as they went and Viv wondered if she would reach the square before Anetherey tackled her again, and she was near the trees when Anetherey's hand fastened on Viv's injured arm. 'Tell me!' she hissed.

The pain was so intense Viv doubled over and then boots appeared in her line of vision, and Anetherey's claw-like fingers were prised off. She heard Anfarena's voice coolly issue orders and as Anetherey's shrieks dwindled into the distance, Viv deduced Anfarena had helpers. She was in too much pain to see who or to resist when Anfarena took her good arm and helped her to a bench.

'You were injured at the festivities?' asked Anfarena. Viv shook her head, having trouble breathing, and if Anfarena expected an explanation, she was to be disappointed. Pain made it hard to speak anyway. 'I beg your pardon for Anetherey's outburst. She has been greatly distressed since the events at Soaich Square last night which, I believe, you also witnessed.'

Viv still said nothing but the pain had dulled enough for her to straighten. Anfarena was composed, but her amethyst eyes shared Anetherey's brittleness. 'Anetherey has described the creature to me, *in detail*, and others have described your reaction, *in detail*, so we needn't waste time debating what he is, or whether he is known to you,' said Anfarena.

'The Daimon have waited for the Angellus's return for untold zadicans as have those of us who endure the Vales' barbarism,' she continued, 'and now two Angellus have returned. The Valen's violence has driven one away, perhaps even murdered him and, while the other is injured, she at least, remains.

'Both these Angellus have lately entered The Wheel which means the door our forebears used still exists, can be opened, or was always open but hidden from us. The remaining Angellus can reveal it *if* she chooses.'

Viv was willing to bet that *not* revealing it was not an option. But rifts were not like doors in a compound that

201

always led to a particular room. They could lead anywhere and that *anywhere* could change from moment to moment. Viv had the skills to find a rift, but not to work out where it led and nor, as it had turned out, had Thris.

They had been stuck underground in Hearth Fold, poisoned by Moth Fold's acrid fumes, almost suffocated in Sand Fold, and Thris torn apart in the cat creature's fold. The Wheel had hardly been a picnic either and then there was the little matter of transference. Viv had no idea how many Daimon, Du-Daimon and elddra intended to tramp through *this* door, but arriving en masse in any fold could devastate its inhabitants or prove deadly for the arrivals, or both. 'I'm not Angellus,' she said finally, aware of the inadequacy of her response.

'You might not call yourself that, but you certainly are,' replied Anfarena smoothly.

'My mother was what you call Valen.'

There was a longer pause this time. 'And what would you call her?'

'Australian,' said Viv, intending to muddy the waters. It was pointless claiming she came from *inside* The Wheel, given the number of spies the Daimon had roaming about, but planting doubt about her usefulness might buy her some much needed time.

'And your father?'

'An angel.'

'*Angel, Angellus*,' murmured Anfarena. 'Describe him.'

'Dark red wavy hair now mainly grey, fair skin, purple eyes.'

'And his wings?'

'My father's an Archae which means senior angel. I only ever saw wings on junior angels.'

'And the Angellus who escaped the wagoners?'

'A junior angel from my father's lands.'

'But not the same lands as you?' said Anfarena shrewdly.

'I'm from Australia,' replied Viv, knowing how useless the information was.

'So, there are *two* other lands?'

'There are thousands of other lands.'

Anfarena looked shocked. 'But how can that be?' The muscles in her jaw worked for a moment then stilled. 'But the door you came through, it opens into the lands where you father is?'

'It opened from a land full of sand that, when the wind blows, fills the air so thickly you suffocate.'

'Of course, you could be lying to deny us the door.'

Viv sensed Anfarena hoped she *was* lying. 'My father's blood prevents me lying.'

'I must take advice,' said Anfarena abruptly, and rose. 'But be aware, Violet Iris Vacia, that you are watched. There are *many* in the Vales who love the Angellus as the Daimon do, and that like us, prefer you to remain here, at least for the time being.'

Viv's arm throbbed as she made her way back up the street and while she did not think Anetherey had grabbed her injured arm intentionally, it was a taste of the violence to come if the elddra and their Daimon cohorts were thwarted. And even if they forced her to take them to a rift, she had no idea how many people could transit at a time.

And then there was her deal with Baraghan. He had kept his half of the bargain and freed Thris, and she would keep hers, but he faced the same risks as the Daimon. His best bet was Ezam, which at least had a version of the Angellus, but there were no women there, and she had the feeling it was going to be a deal-breaker. Thris had warned her about the risks of transference, although she supposed Baraghan arriving somewhere alone would not have too much of an impact. *Sure Vivi, like ya dear daddy arriving in ya hometown. No impact at all, was there?*

Viv threaded her way across Axian, cradling her injured arm. A section had been cordoned off with gaily coloured flags and a band played. Patterned lanterns illuminated the couples who executed the intricate steps she had practiced with Ithreya and Poss but Viv did not have the heart to check whether they danced or whether Sehereden did, just set off down the darkened, empty streets of Miraj Quarter.

Why the hell was she still here anyway? She should have left the moment Thris had burst free from the cage. He had probably been bound and drugged in that wagon the entire time she had been here but she had not sensed anything. They had once been bound by a silver cord; was there nothing left?

She dashed the tears from her eyes. God, how she hoped he had found his way back to Ezam, but he might be lying senseless somewhere, too weak to find a rift out. She needed to search for him *now*, to grab her pack and go *now*, except she had made a stinking, bloody deal with Baraghan.

Her stomach was so tight she leaned against a wall and retched. The street was deserted but she stared back the way she had come. Anetherey might have escaped Anfarena again and be ready to pounce, or the traders she had robbed of Lefer might be sliding closer, *or* the traders Baraghan had robbed of Thris, or maybe she was just paranoid.

She forced herself on and was almost to the arsehole's compound when a shadow detached from the wall. 'Not paranoid, at all,' she muttered. The shadow bowed and Viv recognised Baraghan's unacknowledged son.

'I bid you good evening, elddra,' he said politely. 'Baraghan en-Esh-accom hopes you are feeling recovered and would like to remind you of your agreement. He would like to inform you that he will send Caibel en-Esh-accom to await you at the gate at dawn tomorrow. Caibel will escort you to where Baraghan en-Esh-accom awaits.'

Viv nodded. The boy had done a good job to memorise Baraghan's convoluted spiel. 'How will I know this *Caibel*?'

'That's me,' said the boy with a grin. 'I will see you at dawn, elddra.'

Ashdane came to earth so swiftly his momentum carried him almost to the Bokos's door then he stumbled inside and sped along its labyrinthine ways, forcing browsing Archaes of all ranks to leap aside. Ky was in his usual place, with Prime-archaes Serith and Mirek, and jumped to his feet as Ash appeared at speed around a bookcase.

'I fear for Thris,' said Ash wildly. 'I fear he no longer lives.'

'Can you go to him, Ashdane?' asked Mirek urgently. 'Do you need Kydane to come?'

Ash shook his head. 'No … I needed to come *here*.'

Mirek poured him ambrosia but Serith remained serene. 'The Bokos is the heart of Ezam's learning,' he said.

Mirek rounded on him. 'There is a scroll that tells us what to do?' he demanded.

'The Bokos is Ezam's heart,' repeated Serith.

Mirek felt like shaking his friend but Ky's face cleared. 'You mean the Bokos is *at* Ezam's heart, Prime-archae?'

'A heart within a heart,' murmured Serith.

'But empty,' exclaimed Ky. 'I have been to the Bokos's centre, Ash. There is nothing there.'

'Can you take me there now, Ky? I *need* to go.'

Ky nodded. 'Drink your ambrosia, Ash. It is a long way.'

Ky and Ash hurried along in silence, Ky because he counted, Ash consumed by dread. He had heard Thris's heart stop but it seemed incomprehensible Thris was dead, and the bizarre thought came to him that he was dead instead; a white-winged Dane marooned forever between Ezam and Crystal Folds.

The scrolls added to his distress. The shelves groaned with them yet the Host remained ignorant. Even the Archae, closest to transcendence of those still manifest, had no interest in them, the dusty smell telling Ash they had lain undisturbed for eons. And then, with shocking suddenness, the scrolls gave way to empty shelves. 'This is as far as I have ever come,' said Ky.

'It is not far enough,' said Ash. 'We need to go on.'

'I will count again from here,' said Ky, but the shelves had taken on the same feeling as the black stone in Maze Fold and he feared the Bokos was about to be plagued by spectres too. He passed two thousand steps and his heart quickened as he recalled Prime-archae Serith's belief in the auspiciousness of threes.

Two thousand five hundred, two thousand nine hundred and fifty, and then Ash suddenly dashed ahead and Ky sprinted after him. The empty shelves had given way to a circle of golden light and the body of an angel lay at its centre. Ash crouched over him and Ky skidded to his knees beside him. Thris lay prone, wings splayed and so wet, water pooled around his naked body. 'Does he live?' gasped Ky.

'Yes,' said Ash, with a tremulous smile. 'He has come back to us.'

Chapter 28

Not even Tormis or Mereya were in the compound when Viv returned, and nor did they appear later that night. They had obviously joined the rest of the compound at the festivities, or were celebrating with those of their own compound. Poss must be with them too or still with Brithergen's people.

The hall's fire was low and she hefted on more wood as she considered the pretty clothes Sehereden had traded for her and wondered whether Poss wore hers tonight. The feeling of exclusion reminded her of school, where birthday invitations had never included the drunk's daughter, and of the gangs, where her position had always been tenuous.

She could be partying tonight too, she reminded herself, if she had stayed in Axian, but the whole gig revolved around children, and being infertile meant she had nothing to trade. Besides, she was just passing through, wasn't she?

Look on the bright side, Vivi. Ya don't have to argue with anyone about where ya going. Which was true, she supposed, although the arsehole would be glad to be rid of her for a few days and, given the sex-tents, Sehereden had probably forgotten about her.

She helped herself to some tocki and settled near the fire to wait out the night. The warmth eased the ache in her arm but the hall's emptiness pressed in on her. She could have ransacked the place, had she still been a thief, and she wondered if the rest of Esh-accom's compounds were similarly unprotected. Maybe the punishment for robbing compounds was even worse than common thieving, or maybe the arsehole's prestige protected him *or* his lethal reputation.

Caibel waited just inside the gate and the sun broke the horizon as they rode out. She rode behind him and had dispensed with the sling, despite her arm still being sore, because it would slow her if she must take to the air. Caibel carried a pack, which suggested their trek was longer than a day and they had not gone far before he left the track and cut across towards the trees.

It was the same route she had taken on her aborted trip to Tahsin's sett. She did not know where Baraghan waited but the forested lands were hillier than the Eshacade's river flats, and more likely to hold his longed-for *door*. It was the elddras' longed-for door too and Viv wondered whether watchers had already reported she had left the settlement. She could see no one on the track behind them, but even if she could, there was nothing she could do about it. Her task was to find a rift then dissuade Baraghan from using it.

Caibel urged his horse into the trees and Viv dodged branches as they wove between the trunks. They rode in silence which gave her plenty of time to churn over whether to go to Astraal, return to Tahsin's sett, or chance her luck on a rift. It was not a new debate but she was no closer to resolving it.

If Thris lived, he would search for her again, which was the last thing she wanted. The only way to keep him safe was to break the Guideship which meant she would have to see him one last time.

It was close to midday when Viv smelled smoke. 'Is Baraghan near?' she asked. Every time she smelled smoke in the wilds of this bloody fold, things had turned into a crap-heap.

'A bit further,' said Caibel.

'Is this a popular place?'

'*Popular*?'

'Do lots of Valen travel through this forest?'

'The Blackwoods? They keep to the Eshacade, the Ristavals are too rocky. There's more risk of maragh and mercat attack here too, although no one's seen mercats for zadicans.' Viv grimaced. Great, pig-bears *and* mercats, whatever they were.

They rode on and it was late afternoon before they reached Baraghan's camp. He did have a fire but there was no wind so the smoke she smelled had not been his. He had set his maark at the base of rocky slope that looked as likely as anywhere to have rifts, and Viv wondered if his angel blood had guided him here.

He helped her from the horse and bowed formally. 'I'm pleased to see you're healing, Angellus,' he said softly, 'and that you remembered our agreement.'

'I keep my bargains,' said Viv briefly, then Baraghan turned to Caibel and clapped him on the shoulder.

'My messenger's proven worthy of my trust, yet again,' he said jovially. 'I've got something for you,' he continued, and handed Caibel a wooden cylinder like the one Quen had used. 'Keep it safe, Caibel. I'm going away for a time and don't want my compound left empty. This confirms with the Sylds that you and yours can use it in my absence. It tells you where I've left coin for its upkeep too.' Caibel grinned and stowed it in his pack. 'Keep the fire going, will you?' added Baraghan. 'Violet Iris Vacia and I are going for a little walk.'

'Bring anything you intend to take with you,' whispered Viv, as she surveyed the slope.

'Is the door nearby?' asked Baraghan excitedly.

'Possibly.'

He slung his pack over his shoulder and they started up the slope, Baraghan keeping the pace slow and steadying Viv in places, despite his obvious eagerness to be gone. 'This is Stelin Ridge, otherwise known as Stone-hole Ridge; Esh-accom's little slice of icestone country. There's more air than stone under our feet here and thanks to collapses, the air keeps getting bigger.'

'What you call doors are *rifts*,' said Viv softly, as they climbed. 'They're more likely in caves but there's no guarantee there are *any* in The Wheel.'

'You used one,' pointed out Baraghan.

'Yes, but they can close in the blink of an eye and not open again for many zadicans. I've been taught how to find them, Baraghan, but not how to work out where they go. Step into a rift and you could end up anywhere.'

'*Anywhere*?'

'There are thousands of other places apart from The Wheel, and some are deadly. I'll find you a rift, Baraghan, but I beg you not to use it.'

'This is a more interesting undertaking than I thought,' he said cheerfully. 'I thank you for your concern, Angellus, but I've enjoyed a very fortunate life and I don't expect that to change.' He grinned. 'I'm in the mood for somewhere new.'

Baraghan was full of bravado but he had no idea what he was getting himself into, thought Viv grimly. They came to a crevice, the stone crumbling as Viv peered in, but there was no hum and she was glad she did not have to enter. There was a cave further along the ledge and this time Viv did go in and peered up to where light streamed in from cracks in the ceiling. 'Stelin's also known as Break-neck Ridge,' said Baraghan behind her. 'Sometimes the shafts above are easy to see, and sometimes not.'

Right on cue, stones rattled down, making Viv jump, and then she heard voices. Baraghan gestured urgently for quiet. 'The stone carries sounds from all over the ridge,' he whispered. 'The speakers might be away on the other side or close. Best they know nothing about us.'

They went on, climbing steadily, checking caves and crevices as they went. The slope had dips in places, thick with bushes, and as they struggled through them, Viv had visions of the ground collapsing and taking her with it.

It *was* like the icestone country the arsehole had dragged her through but with dense stands of trees. They provided good hiding places, thought Viv uneasily, as did the caves. She tensed as she smelled smoke again, spicy this time, but Baraghan seemed unconcerned, and she wondered whether the smoke wended its way up through the broken stone, all the way from his campfire. Then she sensed a hum, not from the fractured stone, but from the grove behind. She headed that way and the vibration strengthened. 'There's a rift here,' she whispered.

'Where?'

Viv extended her hand. 'Exactly here,' she said.

'Can I use it to leave?'

'Yes, but you shouldn't, Baraghan. It …' Birds broke from the branches and there was the thud of running feet. 'Someone's coming,' hissed Viv.

'Farewell, Angellus,' said Baraghan, and launched himself forward. The air swallowed him but then Viv was roughly thrust aside as a shape rushed past and leapt after him.

'No!' screamed Viv, but Anetherey was gone.

It took Viv a long time to find her way back to Caibel's camp. She was frightened of the fractured ground, that those nearby had heard her scream, that Anetherey had gone to her death. Baraghan had a lot in common with the arsehole which gave him a good chance of surviving wherever he ended up, but not Anetherey.

Caibel seemed neither surprised nor upset that Baraghan had not returned and happy to head back to Esh-accom. It meant riding through the night but Viv wanted to be quit of this place of broken stone and echoing voices.

Caibel packed up Baraghan's gear, tethered Baraghan's mount to his own, and they set off. He sang to himself softly as they rode and Viv was grateful he made no attempt at conversation, her stomach so knotted she felt nauseous. In the parlance of the court system back home, she had *aided and abetted* a massive act of transference, with who knew what consequences, and it was unlikely to be the end of her *misdemeanours*. Anfarena and her Daimon mates demanded the same service and she did not think their patience would last much longer.

The Fire Zadic came and went and they left the trees behind and came back down into the Eshacade's broad valley. Caibel increased their pace and Viv was relieved when Esh-accom's walls emerged from the gloom.

She insisted he leave her just inside the gate, despite his polite protests, and set off on foot into the Miraj Quarter. Dawn was close but hopefully the arsehole's compound would still be sleeping after their night of dancing and

213

other *activities*, and she could slip into her room unnoticed.

But when she pushed the yard gate open, the courtyard was ablaze with light and crowded with horses. Something was amiss and Viv's heart migrated to her throat as she hastened to the building. Voices told her the hall was full of men and, keen to avoid them, she hurried down the passage to her room, quietly opened the door, and stopped.

Poss's bed was empty and Viv's gaze jerked from the wrenched back cover, to the over-turned chair, to the open shutters.

'Viv!' It was Ithreya and Viv's heart thundered as she took in her tear-stained face.

'What's happened?' she asked, sick with dread.

'It's Fariye. She's been taken.'

Anetherey laughed as the perfumed wind whipped the hair from her face. She was being carried along on a wondrous trail of iridescent light and then the trail twinned, and she was swept to her left. It did not matter; all trails led to the Angellus and she would soon be in their glorious company, never again to be parted.

And then the beautiful play of colours ended, and she was thrown forward onto a creamy bed of sand. Anetherey clambered upright and brushed herself down. Great hills of sand swept away in every direction, reminiscent of Astraal's sacred peaks. Beyond their crests would be a lake, as pristine as Astraal's sacred lake, and there beside it, would be the Angellus's blessed dwellings.

She hurried up the first hill, down its other side, and up the next. The lake would be just beyond the next crest, she told herself. She had brought no food or water, word of the Angellus's swift exit from Esh-accom having necessitated her own. It did not matter. Nor did it matter when a breeze woke. The air was mild and the light the same, which meant she had not been there as long as she thought. The Angellus's dwellings would be just beyond the next crest.

Baraghan rode the iridescent tunnel with knives drawn. He saw the tunnel twin, and threw himself to the right, the side of his strongest knife-hand. A circle of silver rushed towards him and then he was tossed out onto solid earth.

He managed to remain upright and dropped into a crouch as he surveyed his surroundings. Leaves rustled musically under his boots, and he gazed in wonder at the soaring forest of gold and silver trees.

The sky was orange, which told him it was sunset, and he straightened, then tensed again, as he heard someone's approach. The stranger was in no hurry as he meandered through the trees. His gaze drifted between their branches and the ground giving Baraghan ample time to observe him.

There was no sign of wings but he was undoubtedly an Angellus: green-robed, grey-haired, and with an odd, dreamy expression that remained unaltered, even when he saw Baraghan.

Baraghan bowed stiffly and waited, but when the Angellus finally spoke, his words made no sense. 'Ah,' he said, in a melodious voice. 'I see it has begun.'

End of Angel Caste Book 4 – Angel Bound

Complete Viv's story in: Book 5 Angel Blessed

Amazon US - https://www.amazon.com/dp/B0788QQVFV
Amazon Australia - https://www.amazon.com.au/dp/B0788QQVFV
Amazon Canada - https://www.amazon.ca/dp/B0788QQVFV
Amazon UK - https://www.amazon.co.uk/dp/B0788QQVFV

Take a peek at Book 5

Viv's wings thrashed as she launched into the air, dropped into the shaft, and landed with a jarring thud. The sound of fighting echoed through the stone *and* the sound of running feet. Viv whirled. Which way? Which way? Then a shadow flashed along the wall in front and Viv gave chase. The man unsheathed his knife as he ran, and his final few strides took him to a cavern, and a huddled shape. Viv leapt onto his back but he barely faltered, just wrenched her off, and threw her against the wall.

Her wings bedded in an instant and as his knife hand swung back, she leapt again, onto Poss this time. Poss's scream was muffled by the gag, and Viv locked her close to form a shield. And then the knife plunged into her back. It knocked the air from her lungs and white-hot pain exploded as he wrenched it free and plunged it in again.

'Poss,' she choked. Poss's screams told her the little girl lived, and she clung to that as she waited for the final strike. It never came. There was a thud, then a crushing weight as the man collapsed on top of her, and then he was gone.

216

Viv managed to turn her head. It was the arsehole, his face contorted with the blackest hatred she had ever seen, his knife bloody as he twisted in the trader's back. She rolled clear, clawed her way upright, and staggered back down the tunnel.

I hope you enjoyed *Angel Caste* Book 3 – *Angel Bone*. **Authors need reviews!** It is how our readers find us. I would love you to leave me an honest review on Amazon, Goodreads, or another of your favourite reader sites. Read on to discover my other books.

Works by K S Nikakis
Available on Amazon KDP and a range of digital platforms.

Non Fiction

Journey: Seeking the Sacred, Spirit and Soul in the Australian Wilderness

Deadway - Finalist Best Poem
2020 Australian Shadows Awards

When we set out into the wilderness, what is it we *really* seek?

Do we seek new sights or do we seek new selves? And are we *really* on one journey or on two?

Journeying fifteen thousand kilometres into Australia's blood-red heart, Nikakis discovers that every journey is perilous, for travellers risk carrying the clutter of their outer lives with them; a clutter that blinds them to the other journey they crave; that of the inner *soul-journey* into a deeper understanding of self.

To enter Australia's vast Outback wilderness, is to enter a place of endless horizons; a place doused with brilliant gold dawns and dazzling sunsets; a place silvered by star-encrusted night skies and, most importantly, a place of hidden sacred places in whose deep stillness our inner journeys can at last unfold.

In the spirit of travellers like Robert Macfarlane and Scott Stillman, Nikakis asks what it is we really see, feel and understand when we follow in the steps of those who have gone before us deep into the wilderness.

Drawing on her Ph.D. in Joseph Campbell's hero myth, and using original poetry and novel extracts, Nikakis takes us on this second journey; a journey of the sacred, spirit and soul, where our inner selves finally have the time and space to gift us richer and more fully-realised lives.

Fantasy Novel Series

Angel Caste 5 Book Series – available complete in one book or as five individual books: Angel Blood, Angel Breath, Angel Bone, Angel Bound, Angel Blessed.

Angel Caste – Complete 5 Book Series - *A modern female hero on a timeless quest*

A troubled street kid, an angel guide, a binding promise . . .

Viv is on day release from jail to attend the funeral of the thug she thinks is her father, when her real father turns up, the powerful angel Archae Kald. If that is not shocking enough, Viv discovers her mother is not dead after all but lost somewhere in the tangle of worlds called the Rynth.

Determined to find the only person who ever loved her, Viv rift transits to Kald's angel world where he assigns the beautiful Thris to guide her to her mother. Thris is different to every male Viv has ever known but after a life on the streets, she finds it impossible to trust.

Thris trains her to travel the rifts, but the Rynth is a dark and dangerous place, even for angels and when Viv's angel traits emerge, disaster strikes. Lost and alone in the Rynth, Viv stumbles on a lost child in a war zone, and pledges to take the child to safety. But in the perilous worlds of the Rynth, deciding who is friend and who is foe is a deadly game of chance.

Bound by his pledge to guide Viv to her mother, Thris embarks on a desperate search for her, but a greater threat confronts them both and they must fight not just for their own lives, but for the lives of those they love.

The Kira Chronicles - 6 Book Series – available complete in one book or as six individual books: The Whisper of Leaves, The Silence of Stone, The Secrets of Stars, The Thunder of Hoofs, The Crying of Birds, The Music of Home.

The Kira Chronicles – Complete 6 Book Series – *traditional fantasy with deep forests and high stakes*

A gold-eyed Healer, a prophecy, two brothers at war.

In seasons long past, twin gold-eyed princes sundered a kingdom. Rejecting his brother Terak's warrior ways, Kasheron led his people deep into the great southern forests and established the healing settlement of Allogrenia. The Tremen flourished, upholding Kasheron's legacy of peace and healing, and protected by the vast, trackless trees.

All Tremen delight in the healing arts, but Kira is the greatest Healer of them all.

To the north of Allogrenia, drought ravages the Shargh's land, and as their suffering escalates, the chief's younger brother seizes on an ancient prophecy to snatch the chiefship for himself. The prophecy links the Shargh's doom to a gold-eyed Healer, and Kira has gold eyes.

The Shargh attack with devastating consequences and Kira must fight to save the wounded, but the Shargh wounds rot, no matter her skill, and Kira finds herself in a deadly race against time. As the slaughter continues, she makes the horrifying discovery that the Shargh hunt *her*. To halt the attacks and save her people, she sets off for the North to seek aid from her long sundered warrior kin.

But the dangers beyond the forests exceed even the Shargh attacks. The Tremen detest their warrior kin but Terak's descendants have inflicted a worse fate on the Tremen. Kira's new-found love is torn apart by ancient hostilities and when trust turns to betrayal, it risks everything she fought for.

As the battles rage on, Kira becomes increasingly sickened by the bloodshed. Desperate to end the suffering once and for all, she sets out on a quest that could cost her everything and everyone she loves.

Fantasy Novels

The Emerald Serpent – *the Celtic Fae in a fight for survival*

Book trailer: https://www.youtube.com/watch?v=bGpKxnpCEMg

Betrayal, torture, death: Etaine lives on only to destroy those who robbed her of everything she loved.

Seven years before, Etaine met fellow Ranger Cormac, the Eadar she believed was her longed-for true-mate. Emerald-eyed, white-skinned, and black-haired, the Eadar had formed into Ranger bands to fight the Fada, invading religious zealots determined to replace the Eadar's Serpent Goddess with their own gods of stone.

The pure blood of the ancient Eadar runs strong in Etaine and Cormac's veins, and their joining had the potential to open the Emerald and Serpent Ways to them, old worlds only true Eadar can enter. But their love affair goes tragically amiss, with catastrophic consequences.

Etaine flees and as the years pass, slowly rebuilds her life, but the Fada's attacks grow more ferocious, and the Eadar are forced to fight for their very existence. When the Fada mass to commit yet more bloody slaughter, and the bands join in a final, desperate effort to defeat them, Etaine comes under Cormac's command, the very last Eadar she ever wants to see again.

Together they have a weapon that can destroy the Fada, but to use it, Etaine must learn to trust again and Cormac to Remember. And time runs short: the Serpent rises.

Heart Hunter – *a female hunter on an impossible quest*

Fleet is a young Sceadu hunter: skilled, strong, and fast. She hunts deep into the icy mountains, seeking meat for her people, for the rains have failed and plunged the Sceadu into hunger.

Her hunts are hard, but she has much to look forward to. Soon she will be gifted her air-name by the Sceadu's shaman, and then she will be a full adult, and free to marry the man she loves.

But while Fleet is on hunt, the old shaman dies, and the new shaman visions a very different future for her: cross the frozen, ice-locked mountains and complete a perilous quest or lose the man she loves forever.

In a moment of anger and frustration, Fleet commits a terrible wrong and sets out into the frigid mountains to atone with her life. In a journey that takes her deep into the earth's darkest places, into strange new worlds, and even into Death itself, she discovers that only she can save her people. To survive, she must draw on every shred of her hunter strength, and doing the impossible, it turns out, is just the beginning.

The Third Moon – *science fantasy with a very human quest*

Where does the past end and the future begin?

Haunted by inherited memories of his people's dispossession and theft of their children, Warrain is just twelve years old when the nightmare repeats. But Warrain isn't living on Earth in the 21st Century, he is living on the planet Imago in the far flung future.

Five years before, Station One's Mech's got high on the opioid arrash, and in the bloodshed that followed, Warrain's scientific community were expelled from the Station, his father murdered, and his mother and unborn sibling lost to him.

The scientists carve out a rudimentary Station high in Imago's ranges, and Warrain's friends get on with their lives. Not Warrain; he climbs the Tors to stare down at Station One, dream of his mother and sibling, and plot revenge.

And then one day, everything changes. A third moon appears in the sky, one of Imago's life-forms calls him by name, and disease breaks out at Station One.

When the Mechs visit to seek help for their ill, Warrain seizes the opportunity to deal them a blow they will never forget. But the third moon brings changes that threaten them all and, to aid the life-form whose kind is being dispossessed and slaughtered, he must turn his

back on the hate that has long sustained him and find
another way to live.

Messenger – *a dystopic future filled with hope*

In a world made deaf by hatred, who will hear the messenger?

Severine's world ends the day her family is murdered. Being raised in the loving community of gay Travelers always marked her as an outsider, but being female puts her in mortal danger. Women are scarce, precious, and hunted.

When chance brings Severine face to face with the father she has never known, he assigns the son of his murdered best friend to guard her. They soon clash. Severine believes all men are violent brutes and Jeph resents his freedoms being curtailed.

An uneasy understanding grows but Jeph is glad to deliver her to the Enclaves, a sanctuary her father has carved out in the mountains for his women and children. But there is no safety in a world broken by war and sickness and when violence follows her, Severine flees to the northern city of Andhaka in search of a home amongst her mother's people. Jeph follows, bound by loyalty to her father, but the north holds terrible dangers for him.

It's been years since Andhaka has welcomed outsiders with anything but bullets, and to survive and to protect Jeph, Severine must learn to use her enemies' weapons against them. As the stakes rise, she comes to understand the horror of her mother's loss, and what drove her father north seventeen years before. His quest becomes her quest, but she hasn't counted on the savage legacy that war and sickness have left behind, or on falling in love.

I Heard the Wolf Call My Name – *gender-fluid shifters in search of home*

Finalist Best YA Novel – 2019 Aurealis Awards

Jax is just twelve years old and in bird-form high above his island home, when it explodes, killing everyone on it. He believes he is the only survivor until ten years later, he comes face to face with his boyhood friend, Matiu.

Matiu is military and the military need shifters for a crucial mission, but Jax refuses. Having spent ten long years burying his bizarre shifter past, he isn't about to resurrect it. But Matiu rouses other feelings too that Jax finds harder to ignore.

As the military ramps up pressure to force Jax's cooperation, he shifts to bird-form and flees to the last remaining island where he crash lands in the middle of Anahera's vision-quest. She searches for her skin-spirit animal to transform her into a protector of her people, and dreams of finding the white-wolf, but finds Jax instead. To save him she must abandon her quest but her kindness only adds to Jax's turmoil.

To decide who he truly is and where he really belongs, he must first confront his painful past, but that isn't the worst of his problems. The forces that blew Jax's island out of existence now threaten Anahera's as well, and he might just be the only shifter who can save it.
And time is running out.

Fantasy Short Stories

The Gift – A Deep Fantasy Short Story #1 – free on my website at www.ksnikakis.com

Excerpt:

Thariel sat for a long time, surveying all around her, as if she ate the world that would soon be memory. Then she took the harness from the mare, and with soft words, thanked her and bade her farewell. Her own feet she turned towards the forest, tossing her face-plate aside as she went, so that her hair fell loose to her waist, then she discarded her chest-armour, the sword and dagger, her bow and quiver.

The trees closed in and she came at last to the lake Men call Menios and stood for a while on its shore. An owl cried and a mouse shrieked, and all around her the souls of the newly dead jostled in their journey to the void. She stepped into the water and the new life inside her quivered.

'Fear not, little one,' she whispered, in her own tongue. 'We are going home.'

The Tale of Prince Anura – A Deep Fantasy Short Story #2 – free on my website at www.ksnikakis.com

Excerpt:

I should have been happy, for she was beautiful. Dark rivers of curls, skin as white as moonlight on water, breasts softer than spawn, and she loved me well. But her chamber was small, no matter the comfort of her bed, and the old feelings of entrapment rose, as persistent as gas that bubbles from rot below still waters.

I sat at the casement and listened, as I had once loitered near the watery skin of the second world and waited. The moon grew large and small many times, but it came at last, as I knew it would. The soft lament on the night-time air, the song of a soul as confined as mine. It took me a journey of many days through the depths of a massive forest to find her tower.

Stone it was and sheer, and as remote as the third world's glimmer had once been. I sang to her and she answered with sweet melodies of her own and we made love as frogs do, with our voices. And when trust had built, she let down her shining ladder of golden hair.

Glass-Heart – A Deep Fantasy Short Story #3

Finalist Best YA Short Story, Aurealis Awards, 2019.

Excerpt:

Geth moved amongst his band, exchanging quiet words while they waited. Some he had fought with since the Tallon's foul ships had first found their shores while others had come later, when the burn of cot and kin had sent them from their valleys.

Hate drove them but hate was no shield against arrow and knife. It was fighting skills that kept them hale, and Geth ensured they had them aplenty. He needed them living, not just for their own sakes and his, but for what would come later. When the Tallon's stain had been scoured away, the destroyed must be rebuilt.

Kyth sat alone and he went to her and gazed about. 'The glass-heart's fled, has it?'

'I sent her to a place of safety. She will come to me when it is over.'

'Safety was what I wanted for you!'

'And what I wanted for Nyar.' Her eyes caught the star-sheen as she looked up at him. 'But you can't always have what you want, can you, Ceannasai?'

Dragon Sprite – A Deep Fantasy Short Story #4

Excerpt:

Genn rocketed straight upwards, not just because she enjoyed seeing the limitless blue sky before her, but because a Waiwin's wing shape made vertical flight harder for them. Orin didn't try to catch her but swept in circles around her, gaining height in an ever-narrowing spiral. It was a clever tactic and one Genn didn't believe hehad thought of in the instant she had cleared the trees. He had obviously studied her strategies and developed a plan to counter them *or so he thought*.

Genn waited until the spiral narrowed to *axeel*, the minimum distance a Waiwin must keep from a Velven unless she *accepted* him, then swerved towards him, narrowing the distance between them. Orin's eyes flashed to black, shocked she *had* accepted him, but before he could act, she folded her wings and dropped.

The strength that had driven Orin's pursuit had surged to his wing-tendrils in anticipation of locking them with hers and he would struggle even to stay airborne until it flowed back.